"Get out of my car."

Char reached across Eli to open the passenger door. Her body touched him— that is, her wool jacket pressed against his thermal sweatshirt, which covered a couple of other layers. There was nothing sexual in the touch. Nothing sexual between them. Only anger and hurt on her part, and confusion and desperation on his. No reason in the freaking world for him to kiss her.

But he did. Hard, fast, deep, hot. And what flared to life like a fire carefully banked in a stark, barren hearth made less sense than anything that had happened so far. But, man, it felt good. It felt real. Like a lifeline that would keep him from falling into the bone-deep despair that had been his father's ruin.

And how could Eli ever have known that someone from his past would feel so right in his present?

Dear Reader,

I came late to the romance genre table. As an opinionated college student, I had a preconceived, utterly baseless and unflattering opinion of paperback romance novels. I didn't read "those" kinds of books.

Then I got married, had two babies and found myself craving multisyllable words. I still loved to read but didn't have the time or money to devote to "serious" hardbacks. My beloved mother-in-law, Mae Salonen, took a chance and handed me a grocery sack filled with Harlequin novels.

To my surprise, the stories were rich, diverse and wonderfully entertaining. The characters were larger than life, true to life and "my life" all rolled into one. The authors inspired me with hope, humor and, of course, love.

Now I'm doubly blessed. Not only do I get to *read* stories that take me into new worlds with interesting people, I get to *write* stories that create these worlds. Take Sentinel Pass, for instance. Char, the heroine of this book, woke me from a dream one night to say, "I'll tell you something about me you don't know— an old black woman lives in my head." I was hooked. Eli was a dream of a different kind.

I thank my cousin, Linda Thompson, an accomplished Lakota bead artist, and her lovely daughter, Donna Ducheneaux, for answering my questions about Lakota life—all mistakes are mine. And to Linda's son, Damien—thank you for lending me your name and providing a source of inspiration.

And thank you, Harlequin, for sixty great years!

Debra Salonen

Finding Their Son
Debra Salonen

HARLEQUIN®

TORONTO • NEW YORK • LONDON
AMSTERDAM • PARIS • SYDNEY • HAMBURG
STOCKHOLM • ATHENS • TOKYO • MILAN • MADRID
PRAGUE • WARSAW • BUDAPEST • AUCKLAND

Recycling programs
for this product may
not exist in your area.

ISBN-13: 978-0-373-78333-5

FINDING THEIR SON

www.eHarlequin.com

Printed in U.S.A.

ABOUT THE AUTHOR

There was a time in Debra's life when she told people she was part Sioux Indian. A six-year-old who spends part of the summer with her aunt and uncle and brown-skinned cousins on an Indian reservation in the middle of South Dakota has got to be part Indian, right? So she claimed—until her mother explained otherwise. "Your aunt is your father's sister, so that means…" Yeah, whatever. But deep down, Deb's love of the Lakota remains intact, and secretly she still wishes she could claim part of this wonderfully rich, proud and complex heritage.

Books by Debra Salonen

**HARLEQUIN
SUPERROMANCE**

1196—A COWBOY SUMMER
1238—CALEB'S
      CHRISTMAS WISH
1279—HIS REAL FATHER
1386—A BABY ON THE WAY
1392—WHO NEEDS CUPID?
      "The Max Factor"
1434—LOVE, BY GEORGE
1452—BETTING ON SANTA*
1492—BABY BY CONTRACT**
1516—HIS BROTHER'S SECRET**
1540—DADDY BY SURPRISE**
1564—PICTURE-PERFECT MOM**

*Texas Hold 'Em
**Spotlight on Sentinel Pass

SIGNATURE SELECT SAGA
BETTING ON GRACE

**HARLEQUIN
AMERICAN ROMANCE**

1114—ONE DADDY TOO MANY
1126—BRINGING BABY HOME
1139—THE QUIET CHILD

This book is dedicated to my aunt and uncle,
Helen Robson Thompson and the late
J. W. Thompson, who welcomed me to their
home on the Lower Brule reservation every
summer of my childhood. There I learned to ride;
I swam in the wide Missouri; and I explored the
beautiful hills and gullies of the Little Bend.

Uncle Jiggs was a gifted storyteller...
like Eli's grandfather in this book.

Helen, your unconditional love was a blessing on
all the children who passed through your doors.

You'll never know what an impression you left
on a young girl with a big imagination
and even bigger dreams.

PROLOGUE

NAKED AND SHIVERING in the mid-November cold, Eli took a deep breath of sage-scented air and forced himself to precede his patiently waiting host into the *inipi,* or sweat lodge.

The darkness was immediate and blinding. He stumbled slightly, relying on guidance from the old man everyone called *Lala,* Lakota for grandfather. "Sit, my boy," the man said in the Lakota tongue.

Eli understood at what must have been a cellular level since he'd never been formally educated in the language of his father's people. He sat, forcing his eyes to open as wide as possible. He assumed they'd adjust to the darkness in a moment or two, but as he looked into the saturated black heat he couldn't make out a single shape or form, although he sensed others were inside the lodge, which was constructed of willow boughs bent and tethered to the ground to make a dome topped with tarps and blankets.

He'd attended sweats before but never like this.

Those had seemed informal, more or less open to anyone. Even him. An outsider of two dozen years. More or less.

"You must complete *Hanblecheyapi*," his uncle had told him, using one of the traditional names for the experience most people called a vision quest. For two days Eli had fasted in the company of strangers. Men who belonged to other tribes, who came to this place for different reasons. He'd welcomed the fast as a way to offset the effects of the copious amounts of alcohol he'd drunk since his life imploded. Then, at the last minute before the ceremony was to begin, his uncle had taken him aside and invited Eli to share a pipe.

Knowing the smoking of the pipe was sacred to the Lakota—on par with the Christian ritual of communion—Eli had trusted his uncle not to spike the bowl with anything other than tobacco or possibly a bit of sage. He'd relaxed his rigid self-control, trying to get into the spirit of the moment. He'd allowed himself to be stripped and anointed with sage. All because his uncle claimed Eli's life was in a shambles.

"You are missing pieces of yourself, nephew," Joseph had alleged.

And how could Eli argue? He was missing a wife and the three—no, two—children they'd made together.

"It is time," a voice said. "To put your fears aside and trust in the Great Spirit." The darkness was so thick and the steam so suffocating Eli couldn't say for certain whether the voice came from a real person or from inside his head. "Accept what is before you."

He closed his eyes and inhaled deeply. Moist heat and the scent of his own sweat blended with sage created a swell of awareness and energy that vibrated and expanded throughout his whole body.

Suddenly a flicker of light appeared, a slim orange reed, dancing like the flame of a candle. He watched, mesmerized, as a tiny, black-capped bird darted in and out of the flickering image. A yearning so deep and elemental it seemed to start in the primal center of his being made him reach out. Hot tears scalded his skin and dropped like pellets of lead on his lap.

He opened his eyes again but nothing changed. Friendly and openly curious, the small bird flitted just beyond his fingertips. *S'kipicickadee.* The brave little bird of tribal lore that was reputed to know the truth. If he followed where the chickadee led, he might finally see his life clearly, no longer allowing his mind to be deluded by what he wanted to see.

That was when Eli knew his true quest had begun. At long last, he would learn the answers to the question he'd never dared ask: Who am I, really?

And if the answer was as disappointing as he feared it might be...well, there was always his father's way. He could drink himself to death and alienate everyone who ever loved him. The past few weeks had proven he'd learned that lesson all too well.

CHAPTER ONE

CHAR JONES HAD TIME to kill.

This almost never happened. She was a busy entrepreneur. *Entrepreneur.* The word tended to make her giggle—something she didn't do well. She also didn't idle away precious daylight. Waiting went against her grain, but she wanted to hold off filling the balloons for Megan's birthday party until the last minute.

Silly, really. Mylar balloons could usually be counted on to hold air for six to ten hours. Much longer than a five-year-old child's attention span. But Megan McGannon was Char's best friend's niece, and balloons could make or break a party at that age. Char took her responsibility as bearer of the balloons seriously.

That meant she had half an hour to fill.

She drummed her fingers on the glass countertop and looked around.

The store was a shoebox-shape cedar log building with a green metal roof that had been built from a kit in the mid-seventies by a pair of hippie artists who'd lived in the double-wide mobile home—where Char presently lived—behind the store. They'd used the home's two-stall garage as a studio. According to local lore, the couple financed their artistic endeavors by growing and selling pot. After they went to jail, the place changed hands several times before Char bought it, erected her trademark white teepee, which served as the building's main entrance during the summer months, and changed the name to Native Arts.

This is silly, she thought. There were a thousand things she could do. "Like dust," she muttered. "My favorite thing." *Not.*

Stifling a sigh, she grabbed the textured yellow cloth from under the counter and walked to the nearest display.

Grace Yellowhawk had an amazing gift for pairing fragrances and fabric. Char had been thrilled to carry Grace's potpourri, dream sachets and unique line of handmade soaps. She picked up a pale pink, heart-shaped sachet and held it to her nose.

Rock rose, she thought, inhaling deeply. A memory from her childhood flitted through her mind. She closed her eyes and pictured warm sunshine on her upturned face. A gentle hand on her shoulder reassured her that the loud, perplexing turmoil coming from inside the house had no bearing on her. Her grandmother? Maybe. Char couldn't remember. But when her grandfather had been alive, visits to her grandparents' home in Pierre had been punctuated with anger, disappointment and tears.

She efficiently swiped the dust cloth over the shelf, restacked the bars of scented soap and fanned out a display of stamped hand towels. She stepped back to survey her work. "Nice."

Satisfied, but still oddly fixated on the shadow memory, she was caught off guard by the sound of a car door in the distance. She pivoted on the heel of her pink and silver running shoes to look toward the parking lot. The floor-to-ceiling picture windows that bracketed the store's front door would have afforded a good view if not for the various displays and the post-Halloween sales banners.

She squinted, trying to make out the driver of a newer model pickup truck that looked vaguely familiar. But a second later, the vehicle took off, churning up a small cloud of dust as it exited the parking lot.

Char was used to seeing people stop and go without coming into the store. Native Arts was located at the junction of Sentinel Pass Road and one of the main north-south highways bisecting the central Hills. Not only did the large, open driveway and parking lot make for a convenient meeting place, Char's big white teepee made the rendezvous spot impossible to miss.

She might not have given the truck another thought if not for the passenger it dropped off.

"Hmm." She sidestepped for a better view, but the person was too far away to see much detail. A man. Tall. Not skinny, but not fat. Not a typical hitchhiker because he didn't appear to have any kind of luggage. The lack of a backpack with a rolled sleeping bag at the top told Char he wasn't headed toward either of the prime Black Hills hiking trails in the vicinity. His boots looked rugged enough, but a bulky black sweatshirt—even the kind with a hood—wasn't adequate protection from the extremely changeable weather at this time of year.

She was pretty sure she'd heard the morning weather report mention the possibility of snow in the next day or two. She watched the man stand unmoving, as if rooted to the spot, for another minute or so. *He's probably waiting for someone to pick him up.* Wife. Girlfriend. Boyfriend, she thought with a rueful chuckle.

Shrugging, she quickly returned to her desk behind the counter. She tucked the cloth back where it belonged and walked to the flat-screen monitor in an area her assistant, Pia, called the "Bat Cave."

A composite image from four security cameras

let her keep an eye on things. The upper left showed the parking lot in wide-angle. The hitch-hiker was a shadowy form barely visible. Across the bottom were two views of the main showroom floor. The last gave a bird's-eye view of the interior of the teepee, which was "attached" to the main building by a utility corridor that included a handicap-accessible restroom. Although Char kept the teepee stocked year-round with mostly low value items, clothing and children's toys, shoppers were less likely to linger in the bright, interesting structure during the winter months since it had proven so difficult and expensive to heat. Char had even resorted to hanging two, colorful Navajo rugs across the opening leading to the adjacent corridor to keep the warm air in the main building.

She studied the monitor a moment longer then turned to the stereo unit squeezed between the TV screen and the cash register. She fiddled with her iPod until she found the folder of instrumental music she wanted. She smiled as Brulé, a Lakota band with a New Age sound, filled the room. Char normally could count on the group's serene and evocative sound to calm her.

Normally.

Not today, it seemed. She drummed her fingers on the counter, staring at dust motes. Her mind returned to the hazy memory of her grandmother's garden. Maybe it was pure fantasy, but she could picture herself sitting under a decaying rock feeder, trying to be as still as possible so the tiny birds, white with shiny black heads, would hop near. She blinked rapidly, suddenly overcome with an intense yearning, a strange sadness.

"What the heck is wrong with me?" she murmured under her breath, idly fingering the hand-beaded medicine pouch hanging from a tether around her neck. Her fingers squeezed the fabric to make out the shape of the object inside the pouch. A key.

"Damn."

Had it been the scent of the rock rose that set her on the path down memory lane today? She'd read somewhere that a person's olfactory sense was the strongest link to memory. Or had the compulsion been lurking in her subconscious for days, waiting for a quiet moment to reveal itself?

She couldn't say, but she knew from experience that sooner or later, she'd give in to the need to reexamine her past. So why not get the trip down memory lane over with?

Resigned, she dug out the tiny brass key and stepped to the middle of the counter. On a shelf at knee level rested a fireproof safe about the size of a toaster oven.

"This is such a bad idea."

But once the safe's door swung open she stopped berating herself. Nestled inside the thick walls rested the dozen or so cheap, lined notebooks she'd accumulated over the years. She wasn't worried about losing them to fire, but she didn't want her most private thoughts to fall into the wrong hands—or any hands other than her own.

On top was the only one that resembled an actual diary. It had been a gift from one of her aunts on Char's twelfth birthday. The pink leather sported a black poodle with a rhinestone collar— not unlike the one Megan's dog, Bella, wore.

"Megan." Char looked at the clock again.

Still time, she decided.

She nudged the diary aside after sticking the metal tongue of the clasp back into the broken lock. She'd lost the itty-bitty key years ago. Not surprising since she was thirty-three now.

She lightly touched the stack of eclectic spines—wire, plastic, hard binding and soft. Like a divining rod to water, her fingers overshot then backtracked to one particular book.

She closed her eyes and let out a long, resigned sigh. One quick peek, she told herself. After all, Pia might arrive early.

Her conscience made an all-too-familiar tsking sound…which Char ignored. She quickly withdrew the notebook of choice and closed the safe, but before standing she paused to take a deep, calming breath. As she did, her gaze fell on the air pistol strapped to the underside of the counter above the safe. She'd never used it for protection, but she liked knowing it was there.

Sorta like her journals. She could go for months without reading any of them then suddenly she'd need a fix.

She stood and placed the hundred-page, blue-lined composition book faceup. The retro cover sported big neon-pink and yellow flowers. She couldn't imagine why she'd choose something so gaudy. Possibly one of her aunts had given it to her. Her mother had been involved with Devon at the time, and the aunts had provided most of the things their sixteen-year-old niece needed.

Except birth control. Nobody had thought about that.

She glanced at her watch. She had time to skim a few pages—most of which she knew by heart.

Or you could write something new, chickadee.

Char mutely groaned. The voice had been mysteriously absent for a good week, but now it was back.

"Go away."

Char looked around to make sure no one else was present. Talking out loud to oneself was bad enough, but talking to an imaginary voice that spoke with a Southern accent and the dialect and inflection of an old black woman took *odd* to a new level.

Oh, stop yer stallin' and git this over with so we can go to the partee. Morgana Carlyle's s'posed to be there.

Char rolled her eyes. She didn't understand the old black woman's fascination with celebrities. But even as a child growing up in movie star–free South Dakota, Char—and her very vocal conscience—had been titillated by stories of the rich and famous. A fascination that turned up-close and personal when Libby married Hollywood heartthrob Cooper Lindstrom.

Coop's ex-wife and costar, Morgana Carlyle— aka Morgan James—was the latest celeb to fall for a Sentinel Pass local. According to a reliable source—Libby—Morgan and Mac McGannon were "in love."

Le's go, chickadee. Le's get this trip down mem'ry lane over and done with.

Char had racked her brain over the years trying to figure out why her conscience spoke in a stereotypical voice so far outside Char's personal frame of reference. She'd even invented a genealogy assignment in one of her classes to get her aunts to open up about the Jones's family history, thinking perhaps some long-dead ancestor had been a slave owner. But both Pam and Marilyn had clammed up as if such knowledge was a state secret.

"We come from dirt-poor farmers," Pam had

told her. "They weren't the kind to take photos or keep records. I don't see any reason to start now."

Char took that to mean none of her forebears had ever lived in the South or employed a maid/housekeeper/nanny—black or any other color. Yet this was the voice she'd heard in her head for almost as long as she could remember. She'd even written about it in her journal.

Thumbing to a familiar spot, she read:

The old black woman is back. Maybe she never left. But if that's true, then where was she when I needed someone to say, "This is a really bad idea, Charlene. One you're going to regret for the rest of your life.

Char wished she could have blamed all her bad decisions on someone else—even an imaginary voice. Too bad life didn't work that way.

Before she could resume reading, the phone rang.

"Native Arts. Char speaking."

"Hi. It's me, Libby. The party's starting. You're still coming, right?"

Pregnancy had turned Libby into an even bigger mother hen. "Of course. I'd never break my promise to Megan. I'm waiting for Pia to get here before I fill the balloons."

"Great. Morgan is going all out to make this party perfect."

"Why? Is the paparazzi invited?"

Libby laughed. "No, thank goodness. I think we left them all in California this time. But this is Morgan's first attempt at organizing a little girl's birthday party and she wants to do it up big."

Char wondered if that was for Megan's sake or Mac's, but she didn't ask. Mac had been through a lot in the past year. If anyone deserved a second chance at love, it was Mac.

Unlike me.

She tapped her finger on the cover of her journal, knowing the reason behind her fall from grace was detailed on the pages in this book.

"Tell her not to worry. I'll be there soon with a big bouquet of balloons in tow. I promise."

In the background, Char heard the loud, joyous peal of children's laughter. A lump formed in her throat and she could barely mumble a goodbye. Her fingers trembled slightly on the edge of the notebook but she couldn't bring herself to open to the pages she had earmarked.

Well, chickadee? Are you gonna read it or not?

"Chickadee," Char murmured. A nickname given to her by her father, Charles Ballastrad. Seed salesman by day, front man for a band called Chick Ballastrad and the Guys by night.

The Guys were losers, her mother always said. Char barely remembered her father. Her parents divorced when Char was six, and, tragically, her father and two band members were killed three years later in a bus accident after a gig in Minnesota. Char's mother took back her maiden name and changed Char's at the same time to help them both "move on."

Nobody called her chickadee after that.

Except the old black woman in her head.

Char opened the notebook, surprised, as always, by the meticulous penmanship.

Mom's in love. Again. His name is Devon, but she calls him D. Short for divine. He isn't. Not even close. I don't know why she can't see what a creep he is. Even the old black woman agrees he's trouble.

Char licked the tip of her finger to flip ahead in rapid succession. She didn't need to read what came next. To this day, she couldn't be around a bonfire without picturing the entire scene unfold in front of her eyes. The *Hustler* magazines. The trash can. The flames that jumped far higher than she'd expected after she tossed in a match.

She skimmed to the bottom of the page.

Devon moved out this morning. Mom's not talking to me. She stopped crying long enough to say it was *all my fault*.

Char sighed. Her troubled relationship with her mother had gotten more troubled after that. Pam might have been more supportive if she hadn't been so upset about the smoke damage. Only the old black woman took Char's side.

What kind of man leaves his dirty magazines around for his girlfriend's daughter to find? A man who got hisself a problem. That's who.

The sudden and unexpected tinkle of the bell over the door made Char slam the notebook closed. Her heart rate spiked guiltily. "Hello," she called out, looking left and right, trying to spot the new arrival. "Welcome."

A man.

She rose on her toes.

The man from the road.

She looked over her shoulder. Sure enough, the solitary figure who had last been standing near the highway was gone.

Hmm. She didn't believe in prejudging people— a guy driving a Lexus might be just as dangerous as a fellow on foot—but it suddenly struck her that she was alone and help was several minutes away.

She reached under the counter to reassure herself that her pellet gun was there.

"May I help you?" she asked, pleased by the relative calmness in her voice.

The man stumbled slightly, nearly knocking over a rack of greeting cards by the door. "No… um…no, thanks."

She let go of her journal and reached for the portable phone. She had 9-1-1 on speed dial, just in case.

He edged a bit farther into the shop, veering to the left toward the book display. She looked at the monitor again. *Damn.* A rainbow arch of multi-size dream catchers obscured her view of him, but what she saw confirmed her earlier impression— no backpack and not enough warm clothes.

Maybe the guy's ride stood him up, she thought. Her heart rate started to return to normal. Being stranded on the road didn't make him a bad person. Generally she'd learned to trust her instincts where strangers were concerned, and at the moment her radar didn't feel threatened.

"There's coffee and cookies on a table near where those Navajo rugs are hanging," she told him.

His low grunt brought to mind her grandfather, a loud, vitriolic figure who passed away shortly after Char and her mother moved to Pierre. Unfortunately Char's sainted grandmother soon followed.

Char followed the man's slow meandering on the screen. She'd scoffed when her friend Jenna first broached the idea of setting up in-store surveillance. But after Jenna's family's business, the

Mystery Spot, got vandalized, Char decided to invest in a scaled-down version of the same system. Now the unit didn't seem so frivolous.

When she saw him stop beside the refreshment table, she went back to her reading. Helping a traveler in need was supposed to be good karma—something she could always use.

Keeping one ear primed for anything suspicious, she quickly flipped ahead. Her mother's anger had turned to depression, evidenced by her nightly visits to the bar.

I hid Mom's car keys. She knew it, but she didn't get mad or nothing. Instead she smiled all pretty and sweet and said, "The weather is so nice I believe I'll walk to Frenchie's." She didn't get arrested for drunk driving but she wound up with a big cut on her knee from falling down. Aunt Pam made me give Mom back her keys.

Char used to wish that her life was more like the Brady Bunch, but following the Hollywood gossip magazines was a good way to see that acting in a fake perfect life didn't mean your real life was guaranteed to turn out well. And there were so many things you had not an ounce of control over. Like the size of your breasts.

Pam took me shopping for school clothes
'cause Mom was hung over. I went up another
bra size. Pam said I inherited my grandma's
bosom. Great. Just what I need. A crazy voice
in my head *and* big boobs. Life sucks.

Char didn't actually remember writing any of
the diatribes she could point out from her
freshman year, but she had a deep abiding
sympathy for the girl who felt ugly, different and
odd. Big hair had been the rage in Pierre at that
time, and, unfortunately, Char's hair didn't have
the first clue how to behave.

As for her figure… She skimmed down the
page until she found what she was looking for.

Are they ever going to stop growing? I asked
Pam about getting surgery and she yelled at
me. Said I needed to accept who I was and
not try so hard to fit someone else's idea of
who I should be. She didn't even listen when
I told her Becky Halverson said someone
drew a picture of me on the bathroom door
in the boys' locker room. When Bec told me
what they were doing when they looked at
it, I nearly puked.

She slammed the journal shut. She didn't
know why that still got to her. Was it unpleas-

ant being the butt of a joke? Of course. But that had been seventeen years ago. *Get over it,* she told herself. She had a business to run. Balloons to fill.

Instead of walking to the helium tank, she leaned as far to the left as possible, trying to spot her lurker. He'd left the refreshment table and was now hanging around the display of authentic reproductions of early Native American hunting spears. Carl Tanninger, a rancher down by Custer, had researched arrowhead production and made each piece by hand.

Given their value—and price tags—she'd tethered them to the display with a steel gauge wire locking system. She'd never felt more relieved.

"Um…pretty cold out there today, isn't it?" she asked, feebly attempting to be social. She never pestered customers but most were a bit friendlier than this guy.

His back to her, he asked, "Bathroom?"

"Push your way through the Navajo rugs. The restroom is on your right," she said. Was she thrilled about sending him out of sight? No, but even if he wandered into the teepee there wasn't anything of great value to steal. Mostly summer clothes and kids' things.

Kids. Megan's balloons.

She abandoned her notebook on the counter and hurried to the upright tank where she'd set out the balloons she planned to fill. Gift balloons hardly fit the theme of her store, but she was a retailer first and balloons were good for business. Guys would come in for a balloon bouquet for their girlfriends and wind up buying a nice piece of jewelry, too.

Tinker Bell, first. Char was dying to see the special balloon-within-a-balloon inflated.

She smiled as she watched the little blond fairy take shape. She'd ordered it a month ago for Megan's actual day of birth, but so much had been happening family-wise, Mac had postponed the party by a couple of weeks. Once it was filled to capacity, she clamped the end and attached the wrapped gift that had come with it. Soon, Megan and Tinker Bell would be wearing matching necklaces.

She attached one of the ribbons she already had cut and released the balloon. It bobbled to the end of its tether, but didn't soar away thanks to the extra weight of the present. Still, Char carefully secured the ribbon to the handle of the tank's cart while she filled the next balloon.

She'd managed to inflate all the character balloons—party favors for Megan's friends—and was starting on the solid colors when her customer returned. At first, she thought he was going to head her way, but he took one glance at the balloons and fled toward the pottery.

Fine. Pretty hard to shoplift pottery.

As she filled the last balloon—an extra-large fuchsia one, she noticed her notebook had flopped open. Even from a few steps away, she could see her doodles. Her name and Eli's paired in flowery hearts. Line after line of Eli Robideaux and Char Jones. Or rather, Mrs. Char Robideaux. Did every dumb girl suffering from unrequited love doodle the object of her daydream's name, over and over?

The old black woman had warned her not to pin her heart on the first cute boy who looked her way. But Char had been caught up in something she hadn't expected and apparently had no control over.

She knew what Kat would call it: *swoo*. Kat Petroski, Char's friend who had fallen for the wrong swoo twice, defined it as that indefinable element that makes a certain girl gaga over a certain guy. Love was different, Kat said. That came later…if you were lucky. Swoo was first strike. Wham, bam, damn.

That was how it had been for Char when she first met Eli—an upper classman jock heartthrob who didn't know she was alive. That fine spring day of her freshman year when she literally bumped into him in the hallway of school, every stupid thing she'd ever seen in a movie or read in a book about love, lust and sex hit her square in the chest.

Being a shy outsider, she'd adored him from afar until opportunity—God? Luck? Fate?—had intervened. What happened next was written in black and white on the pages of her journal.

A hissing sound made her fumble slightly as she remembered to cut off the flow of helium before the balloon exploded. Impatient with herself for zoning out, she quickly applied the clamp. Her fingers felt thick and out of touch as she attempted to attach the last remaining ribbon.

"Damn," she muttered the same moment the stranger entered her peripheral vision. He'd probably been standing close by for a second or two, but she'd been so involved in her trip down memory lane she'd overlooked his presence.

"Oh. Hello. Sorry. What can I do for you?"

The hood of his thermal-weave sweatshirt had fallen away and was scrunched around his neck. Chin down, his gaze seemed fixed on something inside the lighted display that separated them. His straight black hair—oily and clumped together in spots as if he'd been wearing a stocking cap at some point—was her first clue to his ethnicity. His skin tone was several shades darker than Char's. That could have been attributed to the sun or the cold wind, but his cheekbones cried Native American. Char guessed him to be her age or a little bit older. Overall, he had an I-clean-up-better-than-I-look-at-the-moment way about him.

He brought his hand up and coughed into his fist. Something in the gesture set all sorts of alarms off in her mind, rendering her fingers useless. The balloon she was holding slipped from her grasp. She made a wild reach to grab it, but the brush of air merely encouraged it to go up, until it reached the ceiling, where it bounced along until becoming trapped in the acrylic dome skylight.

The stranger turned slightly to follow the pink escape artist as it made its brave drive for freedom. In profile, she could see his scrubby black beard. It contained a hint of silver.

The fluttering sensation in her chest grew.

"Hey, do I know—"Her words got stuck in her throat the instant his gaze met hers. Those eyes. She would never in a million years forget those eyes.

Yep, chickadee, that's him, the voice in her head chortled. *Eli Robideaux. The source of all your moanin' and groanin' and weepin' and carryin' on all these years.*

And, if I'm not mistaken, he's here to rob you.

CHAPTER TWO

"I DON'T WANT TO DO THIS, ma'am, but, um... give me all the cash you got and I won't...I won't hurt you."

Eli had been plotting the best way to rob this place ever since he spotted the stupid-looking teepee from the road. The guy who'd picked him up near Hermosa—not something Eli would have done if he'd been a white guy looking at a scruffy, stinky red man—was only going as far as the Sentinel Pass turnoff.

"Hurt me?" the clerk with the odd hairdo repeated.

"I could tie you up if that would help. After you give me the money, I mean." He wasn't making sense. Why would he? He wasn't a felon. Usually he was the one arresting people like him.

The thought aggravated the pounding in his head. "Now. I need the money now."

"Why?"

"Why what?"

"Why are you robbing me? Haven't you caused me enough heartache over the years?"

He shook his head, as if that might rearrange her words in a way that would make sense. Was he supposed to know her? She had to be a good five or six years younger than him. Maybe he'd arrested her once.

"For the record, I'm not robbing you. I'll sign an IOU for whoever owns this place. He's Indian, right? He'll understand."

"She's not Native American," she said, her tone primly politically correct. "She's me. And I don't understand."

Eli swore under his breath. "That old bastard lied to me," he said, swiping at the bead of sweat on his brow. Fever. He'd assumed it was the residual effect of the sweat lodge or his body's way of purging all the toxins he'd put into it. But now he was beginning to suspect his uncle of spiking the water Joseph had slipped him before guiding Eli on the "going up on the hill" aspect of his journey.

His goddamn uncle had tricked him. Eli could only remember bits and pieces of what happened after the sweat lodge, but when he'd woken up this morning in a crappy sleeping bag in the middle of nowhere, fully dressed but shivering so hard his teeth were clattering, Eli knew he'd been the victim of his own stupidity. Whatever made him trust his father's brother—an alcoholic who claimed to hear the voice of the Great Spirit—proved how messed up he was.

"I knew it," he cried, not caring that he was probably scaring the shit out of the woman across from him. He pounded his fist on the glass countertop, making the book she'd been reading bounce off. It landed at his feet, along with half a dozen cheap plastic trinkets. The kind of crap every tourist trap in the state carried. Fake Indian stuff.

That felt like another betrayal, and what little control he still possessed evaporated. He grabbed a wooden stick that was leaning against the counter and swung it overhead. He wasn't planning to hurt the woman but he sure as hell was going to do some damage. He'd take his frustration out on the made-in-China junk peddled for a worthless society that didn't honor vows or truth or—

"Drop the talking stick or I'll shoot."

He'd forgotten the woman with the strange hair was still there. When he spotted the gun in her hand, he froze.

"You don't recognize me, do you, Eli?"

She knew him? *Shit*.

"I'm not surprised. It's been a long time. Pierre High. I was a freshman when you were a senior."

He'd gone to Pierre instead of a reservation school because of his basketball ability. His father's dream had been for Eli to parlay that skill into a full ride at a Big-10 college until…yeah, well, until everything changed.

"What kind of gun is that?"

"A Lugar. Hollow point bullets. The kind that will chop you up inside at close range. So put the talking stick down. Libby would kill me if you broke it."

He lowered his hands, glancing at the gnarled hunk of wood. He knew what a talking stick was and normally would have shown someone's spiritual icons more consideration. At the moment, he was tempted to break the limb over his knee. The only thing stopping him was the fear he'd embarrass himself by not being strong enough to crack it. "Who's Libby?"

"None of your business," she answered saucily. "That's right. Set it down carefully. Now, leave before I have to tie you up and call the police."

He didn't believe her…about the gun. It wasn't a Lugar. And he didn't think she'd shoot him. Women weren't as quick to pull the trigger as men were when faced with the same option. Fourteen years with the tribal police had taught him that. But the way his luck was running at the moment the last thing he should do was test the odds.

"I… Who are you? What's wrong with your hair?"

She put one hand to her head self-consciously. "Nothing. I like color. It's my statement."

"It says you're odd."

"You got that right, but I'm not the one trying to rob a store in the middle of the day. With no weapon and no getaway car. There's odd and then there's dumb."

Dumb. Stupid. Insane. His life had been turned upside down and inside out from the moment his wife tossed him the results of a DNA test and left. Right, wrong. Good, honorable. Truth, reality. Son, not-your-son. None of the words made sense anymore. Which was how Joseph got to him. He'd played on Eli's weakness and sent him off on this foolish journey to nowhere.

Wrong. The minute he'd spotted this place, he recalled Joseph's last words to him, muttered in that strange, singsong tone his uncle used when he was trying to act like a medicine man. "Follow the spirit path to the big white teepee in the shadow of *Paha Sapa*." The Black Hills.

Eli had thumbed a ride from a guy headed north. He'd planned to track down his uncle, who supposedly had a lady friend living near Sturgis. He'd completely blanked out the part about the white teepee until the guy pulled into the parking lot, telling him, "This is as far north as I'm going." The guy had been blathering for miles about meeting his fiancée at a little girl's birthday party in

Sentinel Pass. Like Eli gave a shit about anybody else's kids. His were probably messed up for life and there wasn't a damn thing he could do about it.

Eli had managed to mumble some sort of "Thanks" before getting out of the truck. Normally he had better manners. He would have given the guy his card and offered to return the favor if the man was ever stranded in the middle of the state. Unfortunately that was before Eli's life turned upside down and he grabbed at the damn, spiritual straws his uncle had held out. As if the answer to his problems could be revealed in a hellhole filled with hot rocks and sweaty men at a ranch somewhere on the Pine Ridge reservation.

For a moment there, in the blackness, he thought he'd glimpsed something—someone—that might hold the answer to how his life had gotten so far off track. But the elusive image had fluttered out of sight, like a wild bird, and he'd agreed to give the quest one more try—on a bitterly cold hilltop in the Badlands, where Eli spent one of the worst nights of his life.

He'd awoken that morning, curled in a ball, shivering like a drug addict in need of a fix. No uncle. No car. No money or credit cards in his billfold. Bankrupt in every sense of the word. So desperate he'd stooped to taking what he needed—even though he planned to pay it back someday. And the person keeping him from going on with his journey was someone who knew him.

He looked at her again. There was something familiar about her. She reminded him of the little bird in his sweat-lodge-slash-hallucinogenic induced dream.

"Who did you say you are?"

"Charlene Jones. My aunt was a nurse-practitioner in Pierre. The last time I saw you your cousin, Robert, dropped you off at her place after your bachelor party. You were getting married the next day."

He touched his finger to a little scar mostly hidden by his eyebrow. "Your aunt saved my butt."

She made a scoffing sound. "My aunt wasn't there. She was working at the hospital that night. I stitched your cut. You were my first—and only—patient."

"Why?"

"Why what?"

"Why was I the only one?"

She looked at the book that had fallen on the floor, then made an impatient gesture with the gun. "Just go. Now. My assistant will be here in a—"

From the corner of his eye, he spotted a movement on the screen of the surveillance monitor. A white compact pulled to a stop, and a young woman got out.

Crap. Someone else to witness his fall from grace. He reacted without thinking. He vaulted across the counter and quickly, efficiently disarmed her so she couldn't shoot him in the back as he made his getaway. He was about to dash for the exit that he'd scoped out earlier when the little bell over the door tinkled.

"Goodbye again, Eli."

He froze. He knew that voice. He'd heard it before. But where? He turned and looked at her hard. A hint of memory filtered through the haze in his mind. A gawky girl with pretty, intelligent eyes who hid her voluptuous body beneath funky clothes, her wild hair tucked beneath a crocheted beret.

"Boobs?" he croaked.

Charlene "Boobs" Jones had been a popular source of fantasy for his pals on the basketball team. Eli had had his hands full with Bobbi by that time, but he was honest enough to admit that he might have imagined Boobs naked, once or twice, when he was making out with his less-generously endowed girlfriend and eventual wife.

Her initial look of surprise turned to hurt. "Oh, sure, *that* you remember. Why am I surprised?"

He didn't recall anything else about her. Why

would he? She'd been several years behind him. Her family was odd—to say the least. Plus, she belonged to a past he'd mostly managed to forget. High school went from a stepping stone in a life filled with promise to the high point in a life filled with reality. His dad's hopes and dreams of glory for his only son wound up turning to dust as gritty and choking as dried gumbo—the quicksandlike clay that turned a normal road into a mire of no return. A metaphor that fit his life all too well.

He didn't need any more memories dogging his heels. This whole stupid vision quest was about exorcising the past so he could start over. Start new. Start right. "Well, listen, Boo—um... Charlene, I'm really sorry about this, but I need to borrow some money. Whatever you can spare. I'll pay you back. I promise."

He put out his hand, intending to return the gun and take whatever handout she might offer in exchange.

A sudden, shrill, heart-stopping scream filled the store.

"Damn." He didn't need a degree in law enforcement to know how incriminating this looked to the young woman standing a few feet away, swaying as if she might pass out.

Charlene let out a low groan and shook her head from side to side. He was probably going to go to jail, which meant he wouldn't be able to complete the task his uncle had laid out for him. According to Joseph, if Eli didn't do this right, his kids—his two daughters and the son he'd loved and raised as his own—would never know the man he might have been.

Boobs, er, Charlene suddenly grabbed his shoulders and gave him a little shake. "Go. Out the back door. My car is unlocked, but the key's in my purse so don't think about stealing it. I'll handle Pia."

"I'm not a car thief."

"Good," she muttered. "Here. Take these." She pried the gun out of his hand—a freakin' pellet gun, he realized—and exchanged it for a wad of pink ribbons with balloons attached. "Lose even one and I'll shoot you myself. Now, go."

He was a good cop. He knew how to take orders. He'd never ridden herd on a bouquet of floating balloons, but he'd figure it out as he went. Pretty much the way he did everything in life.

CHAR KNEW THERE WAS NO such thing as coincidence. She'd witnessed enough strange and unbelievable touches of grace in her life and in the lives of her friends to know that Eli Robideaux hadn't stumbled into her store by accident. He was here for a reason, just as he'd landed in her hands that night so many years earlier.

She didn't know what his presence meant or foretold, but he obviously needed her help. And she couldn't say no, any more than she'd been able to avoid what happened between them that night in Pierre.

And you need him, too, chickadee.

She ignored the voice.

"Pia," she said, returning the unloaded pellet gun to its hiding spot. "Deep breaths. Slow and steady. That wasn't what you think."

"He…but…you… I saw… He's an Indian," Pia whispered.

Char didn't have the time or inclination to deal with this young woman's probably deeply in-grained bigotry. Native American tribes and whites in the Black Hills had a long, turbulent history, and while Char did her best to help break down preconceived notions and assumptions, she couldn't dictate her personnel's fears—irrational though they might be.

"Eli's an old friend and I was showing him my gun when you came in."

She hurried around the counter, pausing to grab the folding step stool from the corner. "Here," she said, pushing the two-foot ladder into Pia's hands. "One of Megan's balloons got away. Would you mind catching it while I get my things together?"

Pia hesitated. "You know him? For sure? He looked like a homeless person."

Char snatched her purse from under the cash register and double-checked to make sure her keys were inside.

"We were in school together," Char said, stooping to pick up her journal, which had fallen on the wrong side of the counter when Eli threw his little hissy fit. She stuffed it in her purse and cleared the distance between them. "Eli was Homecoming King when I was a freshman."

Pia didn't look impressed but she did open the stool, march up the steps and grab the wayward balloon's lifeline. She leaned down to hand it to Char. "Here."

Pia, who was in her early twenties and worked at Native Arts solely to flirt with male travelers and earn enough money to fund her shoe addiction, glanced toward the door once more. "Are you sure you don't want me to call the cops?"

"He *is* a cop, Pia. On the reservation." The last she'd heard anyway. "He's on some kind of spiritual quest. I'm going to give him a lift into town after I deliver the balloons to Megan's party. You can handle things here, right?"

Pia shrugged off her trendy, black and gold South Pole jacket. She was a pretty girl with shoulder-length blond hair that behaved like a well-trained show dog. Char's hair belonged in the circus—hence her decision to hide its imperfections with color.

"Is it true Mac McGannon is dating Cooper Lindstrom's ex-wife?" Pia asked, in that breathless tone Char associated with celebrity watching—a popular new sport in this area. More than once Pia had expressed a desire to go to Hollywood and give acting a try. But since she lacked any obvious talent besides her pretty smile and straight teeth, she hadn't gotten far.

Char returned to the cash register and hit the open key. She pulled out the spare key and held it up for Pia to see. "Can you close up for me? I'll probably be back in time, but I'd rather have this covered in case I have to give Eli a lift home. I'll pay you overtime."

Pia brightened. "Really? Cool. Is it okay if I call my friend Molly to come in? It gets dark so early…and, well…you know."

Pia had complained more than once that closing gave her the creeps because the wind blowing across the open hole in the teepee made eerie, moaning sounds.

"Sure. No problem." Char set the key on the counter then removed three twenty-dollar bills from the slot. Normally she would have written a note documenting the cash dispersal, but she knew she wouldn't forget where this money was going. Plus, how would her accountant write off *guilt money?*

After double-checking to make sure the safe was locked, she grabbed her coat. "I've got my cell phone, if you need anything. Thanks. Oh, and…let's keep this little misunderstanding between us. Eli's one of the good guys." *I hope.*

She wasn't banking on her clerk's discretion, but she'd learned a long time ago that she had no control over gossip. Her family had been the focus of all sorts of talk when she'd been growing up—very little of it good.

Ain't that the truth, chickadee. And here you go again. Makin' up for lost time.

Char ignored the comment as she focused on what she needed to do. First, she had to deliver Megan's balloons. Because a promise to a child was not something she'd ever willingly break.

Willingly. Now, that's a word for you. You gonna tell Eli about your promise?

"Eli," she cried with a bit more volume than needed as she dropped into the driver's seat of her Honda sedan. She had a small tussle with the errant balloon, wedging it between her bosom and the steering wheel. "Here. A promise is a promise. I told Megan I was bringing a dozen."

He was slumped down, the hood of his sweat-shirt bunched around his neck. Pia was right. He did look like a homeless person. This certainly wasn't how Char had pictured him over the years. She felt a strong emotion well up in her chest.

Disappointment? Sadness? The end of the dream? No. She hadn't dreamed about him.

Liar. Liar. Pants on fire.

"Do you mind?" she asked, yanking on the balloon's ribbon.

The fuchsia-colored orb smacked him in the face.

He swiped at it with such quick reflexes she didn't realize he had control of the string until she felt it slip through her fingers. The sensation made a tingle race up her spine then quickly radiate through her extremities.

"Brr," she said, trying to explain her shiver.

She turned on the engine and adjusted the heater fan.

"Are the police coming?" he asked, his tone hollow and resigned.

"No."

"Are you taking me to them?"

"I'm going to deliver these balloons to my best friend's niece's birthday party. You can wait in the car while I go in. If you're still here when I come out, I'll drive you wherever you want to go."

His chin came up and he looked at her. "Why are you being so nice? I tried to rob you."

"Let's mark it down to old times' sake."

She backed around the corner of the building then crossed diagonally through the parking lot to the Sentinel Pass highway. A quick glance in both directions told her the road was as empty as her shop had been all day. "Are you hitchhiking?" she asked.

"Yeah. My uncle has my car. I hope," he added under his breath. "I caught a ride with some guy from Denver who talked the whole way. Like I asked to hear his life story."

Jack, she thought, finally placing the truck. "Did he say he was an orthodontist?"

"Yeah. And he's getting married next month. He seemed practically giddy about the idea."

She snickered. "Yep. That would be Jack Treadwell. He's marrying my friend Kat."

The car picked up speed once they'd breached the summit. He put out his hand on the dashboard. She couldn't help noticing the unusual tattoo—an unfinished spiderweb—in the triangular webbing between his thumb and index finger.

"What's that mean?"

"Hell if I know. The old man who gave it to me mumbled something about connecting the dots of my life. I was messed up at the time. Didn't even feel it until the next morning."

"Messed up? You mean like peyote? Cops aren't supposed to do drugs."

He brushed his hand through his thick black hair. Some Native American men of her acquaintance let their hair grow long. Eli's was a slightly shaggy military cut. The hint of silver at his temple was new. And sexy.

Oh, chickadee, are you sure you wanna go down that road again?

"...*wanagi tacacku* or spirit path," he was saying. He made a sound of pure disgust. "Or so Joseph convinced me. He said blood quantum doesn't make you Lakota. And even though I learned to teach the important dances, I'd missed out on the spiritual meaning behind them because I hadn't made a vision quest. Like that was my fault." His low grumble masked a cuss word or two, but she knew he wasn't speaking Lakota because there weren't any swear words in his father's language.

If she remembered her Pierre High gossip correctly, Eli's mother was a white woman from Oklahoma or Kansas. Eli's father worked at the state capitol, and Eli would visit him every summer, spending most of his time with his grandparents and cousins on the reservation.

"My dad didn't believe in the old ways. He called that sort of thing ceremonial crap."

Char remembered hearing talk about Eli's father. Hardworking. Hard-drinking. The latter was something he had in common with her mother.

"Whatever you do," he told her, "don't believe a word Joseph Thompson tells you. My uncle is a liar and a drunk."

"Joseph's your uncle? I know who he is. He worked at the hospital with my aunt. How come he has a different name than you?"

"My dad's father died when he was a kid. Dad had a sister who died, too. Unci—" he said the Lakota word for grandmother with obvious love and respect "—got remarried to the grandpa I knew. They had Joseph and three daughters. Dad and Joe weren't on speaking terms when Dad passed."

Char slowed to make the turn onto Main Street. "I remember your uncle had this long, elegant braid. I was envious because my hair gets to a certain length and breaks off." She shook her head, aware that she was babbling. "Anyway, I take it this means you took part in *hanblecha*. I've never been invited to a vision quest, although I've participated in a naming ceremony and quite a few powwows. Someone mentioned you were teaching ceremonial dance and basketball at the youth center." She kept her tone light to belie her curiosity. "Kind of an unusual combination."

"I quit 'em both," he said without elaborating. "And this wasn't an official ceremony. I agreed to go to a sweat lodge with some of Joseph's friends in Pine Ridge. Joe's getting old. I didn't realize just how badly he's losing it until…"

It was too late, she finished for him in her head. She knew all about those kinds of decisions.

As she drove through the center of town, he sat a little straighter and looked around. "So this is Sentinel Pass, huh? My two daughters love that *Sentinel Passtime* TV show. They think that Cooper guy is a hunk. They say he's going to fall in love with the postmistress and get married and live happily ever after."

He said the last with such disdain she knew all was not right with his love life. "You and Bobbi aren't together anymore?"

"Maybe we never were."

She hated the way her heart did a crazy flip hearing him say that. "Three kids might be hard to explain," she pointed out.

"Two, not three."

"Pardon?"

His elegant black eyebrows drew together above his nose. "How long is this stop going to take?"

Char deliberately slowed the car to a crawl to make her point. "As long as it takes. If you don't like waiting, I can drop you off here," she said, pointing to Elana Grace's corner coffee shop, the Tidbiscuit. "It might get a little chilly in the car, and I'm not so trusting I'd leave the engine running and hope to find either you or the car here when I came out."

"The cold doesn't bother me."

She stepped on the gas. "My friends would

never turn away a stranger, Eli. There'll be food. You look like you could use—"

"I'm fine. I need to get to Sturgis before dark."

"What's in Sturgis?" Not that she had any right to ask, but…

He hesitated so long she didn't think he'd answer, then he muttered two words, "Bear Butte."

Bear Butte was a landmark in the northern Hills that had significant historical and spiritual significance to his people. She'd attended a festival and powwow there a few months earlier with Jordie Petroski, Kat's younger son.

She turned into the cul-de-sac where Mac McGannon lived. There were a lot of cars spread out along the street. She pulled to a stop behind Libby's white SUV and turned off the engine.

"Here," she said, handing Eli the money she'd lifted from her till. "It's not much, but business has been slow since the Hollywood people left. You don't have to pay me back. Like I said, if you want to leave, fine. If you want a ride, I'll be back in half an hour or so. I promised Megan I'd be here and a promise is a promise." The old black woman had taught her that.

He looked at the money but didn't say anything. She wasn't surprised.

She stuffed her purse under the seat. There wasn't anything of value in it—she kept her credit cards locked in her wallet in the glove box. She got out and retrieved the balloons that Eli had shoved into the backseat.

"Thank you."

The low, gruffly spoken words made her smile. "You're welcome."

She was still smiling when she knocked on the front door of Mac's house. Given the din coming from inside, she only hesitated a few seconds before turning the handle and poking her head in. "The balloons are here. Where's the birthday girl?"

"Miss Char." Megan's loud squeal of joy made Char's heart swell as full as one of the helium balloons she carried.

The dark-haired child raced to Char and threw her arms around Char's legs. "You're here. And you brought balloons. They're so beautiful. I love you."

Tears pricked the corners of Char's eyes. She wasn't a crier—ask any of her book club friends—but those three words from the mouth of a child could bring her to her knees. She knew why. Until today, she'd chosen to ignore the reason behind her particular Achilles' heel.

But now, with the cause of this weakness sitting in the front seat of her car, Char knew fate had come full circle. She needed to make peace with her past—one way or another.

CHAPTER THREE

ELI WATCHED HIS RESCUER walk into the average-looking ranch house. Not all that different from the one he'd lived in with Bobbi and the kids since their move to the reservation. Nothing fancy, but he did his best to keep it from falling down around them like some of his neighbors'.

Poverty wasn't something confined to big cities. The people of the plains—particularly people of color, as some liked to say these days—were in a constant battle to stay above the poverty line. Cultural differences that weren't easily explained to outsiders also accounted for the shabby, often run-down, appearance of some houses in his neighborhood.

But the families living in those homes were just people. Probably a lot like the folks Char Jones was now visiting. He'd been to his share of little kid birthday parties. His daughters—Micah, fifteen, and Juline, recently turned twelve—had been social butterflies their entire lives. They also knew a lot of people, thanks to Bobbi's large, extended family and her job at the local casino.

His stomach made a loud, complaining sound the moment the door closed behind Char. He'd sampled one of the cookies Char had left on a plate beside the coffee thermos at the store, but it hadn't done much to fill the void. He honestly had no idea when he last ate a substantial meal. Fasting hadn't sounded like a bad idea when his uncle suggested it—especially after the self-indulgent binge that had brought Eli onto his uncle's radar.

He slid down in the seat and as casually as possible reached for her purse. Women always carried snacks in their purses, didn't they? Gum or breath mints at the very least, he reasoned.

The cloth bag was made of stiff wool and leather. He could tell it had been made by hand. He'd seen others like it at the gift shop in the tribal headquarters.

Keeping one eye on the house, he poked through the usual things you'd find in a woman's purse: cell phone, a package of tissues, a romance novel that had a man, a woman and two kids on the cover. He resisted the urge to throw it in the backseat. He opened a tube of lip gloss because it smelled like coconut. Unfortunately that only made his stomach growl louder.

He spotted the well-worn notebook he'd seen on the floor of the shop but didn't pay it any mind.

"No food," he muttered. "Maybe she's a chronic dieter." Bobbi was constantly fretting over her weight. As if he could tell whether or not she'd put on a couple of pounds.

In an act of pure desperation, he upturned the purse so the contents fell across his lap.

"Aha." He spotted a single stick of foil-wrapped gum. He didn't care if it was a hundred years old—he was eating it.

He unwrapped it and closed his eyes as he laid the stiff, spearmint-flavored chewing gum across his tongue. His taste buds erupted as he chomped down, causing him to smack his lips.

Best damn gum he'd ever had.

After savoring the pleasure for a moment, he began returning Charlene's stuff to the purse. As he reached for the notebook, he spotted something odd. Something familiar that caught his eye. His name surrounded by an elaborate doodle that included hearts and flowers.

"Weird."

He flipped open the page and to his even greater surprise, he found every single line filled with some variation of his last name and Charlene's first name: Char Robideaux, Mrs. Charlene Robideaux, Mrs. Eli Robideaux.

She had a crush on me. He winced, uncomfortable with that kind of adoration. And confused... until he spotted the date on the lower right-hand corner of the page. The year he'd graduated from high school.

Poor, dumb kid. If this notebook had belonged to an adult, instead of a teenage girl, he might have labeled her a stalker. But he'd seen his daughters and their friends develop crushes on boys at school. He also knew that a young girl's fancy was almost always passing.

He hoped Char's crush had been short-lived. To satisfy his curiosity, he flipped forward a few pages, pausing only when he spotted his name. "Yep," he said with a sigh of relief, "hero worship."

Totally misplaced, his conscience added.

He was about to close the journal and stuff the entire bag under the seat where he'd found it when the book seemed to flip open on its own. He skimmed the page.

"No way." He sat up a little straighter.

He read it again, more slowly. "No, freakin' way." He was on his third time when the words finally sank in and he let out a low cry. "This can't be true."

ANY HOPE CHAR MIGHT HAVE harbored that her passenger would go unnoticed by her host and the guests was dashed when Jenna asked, "Who's that in your car?"

"You brought somebody with you?" Kat asked. "Why didn't you invite him in?"

"Uh-oh," Libby said, hurrying to the window. "She's grinning. Char never grins. This is serious."

Libby, founder and rudder of the Wine, Women and Words book club, was uncannily omniscient when it came to her friends' lives. She rarely needed a talking stick to obtain information.

"His name is Eli Robideaux. He's an old friend from high school. He dropped in unexpectedly at the store. He's a little down on his luck and needed a lift."

She thought for a moment she might have pulled it off…until the real actress in the bunch, Morgan, called her bluff. "Nice try. I like the way you mostly stuck to the truth. He's probably all of those things, but your eyes were sparkling when you walked in. That kind of sparkle only comes from one thing." She looked at Kat meaningfully.

"Swoo," Kat cried dramatically. "Char's been hit with a powerful dose. Quick. We have to do something."

Jenna tossed her lush red hair. "Like what? Hose her down with flame retardant? Where's Mac? I heard him mention going back on active duty with the fire department, maybe he can get us some."

"Ha-ha. Very funny," Char said. "If this is swoo, it's seventeen years too late. He's married with three kids. I'm giving an old friend a lift. Period."

A tall, handsome man who had been standing near the front window spoke up. "He resembles the hitchhiker I picked up this morning. Didn't say more than ten words the whole time. Looked like he'd been on the road for days. Smelled like it, too."

Char couldn't deny either observation. "Yeah. Eli needs a bath. That's one reason he didn't come in. He said he's on a spiritual journey, and I gather it started out in a sweat lodge."

Jack strolled over to Kat and put one arm around her. She relaxed against him with a slight purr of contentment—something Char rarely spotted in the busy, single mother.

"Is Jordie here?" Char asked. She hadn't seen the little boy in over a week and needed a fix.

"Out back with the others. Shane and Cooper are in charge of games. Mac's making sure no body bags are needed," Jenna said. "I think it's time for cake, don't you, Lib? Especially since the balloons have arrived."

After greeting Char and giving her a joyful hug, Megan had raced back outside to be with her friends. Char knew that passing around helium balloons outdoors was a good way to lose them, so she'd loosely tied the ends of the bundle to the back of a chair. The large pale green Tinker Bell balloon made a musical tinkling sound when it moved.

"Hi, Char," Mac said, striding toward her—a black and white soccer ball in his hands. "Great balloons. Thanks for bringing them. Miss M," he called over his shoulder, "did you see the Spiderman and Batman balloons Char brought for Tag and Jordie?"

All of the children—six total—rushed to the table, their small bodies pressing against Char. Char didn't recognize the other little girls, but she greeted Kat's boys with a hug and a friendly chuff on the shoulder, respectively.

"Cool balloon," Tag said, snapping his finger against the shiny black and silver image of Batman.

"Spidie," Jordie cried. His slight lisp from the missing teeth he'd knocked out was barely noticeable. "He's my favorite."

Char knew that.

"The Tinker Bell balloon has a special present with it, Megan," Char said.

"Awesome," Megan exclaimed, sounding older than five. "Look, Daddy, see the little box? Can I open it now?"

Mac looked at Morgan for guidance. "Cake first, then presents?"

"Cake."

"Cake."

The chant caught on in a hurry. Char's ears rang, but in a good way. She'd have loved to stay and watch all the excitement, but Eli Robideaux was in her car. The chance of that happening was so remote that it simply had to possess some kind of significance. Without getting all woo-woo, as Jenna would say, Char knew he was here for a reason.

"Meggie," she said, motioning the child to her. "Give me a hug. I'm sorry I can't stay for cake and ice cream, but I have to help a friend."

Megan pouted for a half a second then brightened. "A boyfriend?" Giggling, she put her fingers to her lips as if she'd given away a secret. "Miss Char's got a boyfriend."

Char felt all eyes turning her way. The last thing she wanted was to answer questions that didn't have answers. Not yet anyway. "Have fun with your friends, sweetheart. I'll call you later to see if you liked your present. Bye," she said, fleeing without a backward glance.

Libby would text her before the day was over. Jenna and Kat would follow up, too. They were her friends. They cared about her. But at the moment, she was more concerned about an old friend.

Fur-rend? Don't you be lying to yourself, chickadee. He weren't never your friend.

The old black woman was right. Back then Eli was a god, a rock star and Michael Jordan all rolled into one. He and Char shared the same space in the way the sun and an unnamed asteroid both hang out in the sky. He pretty much confirmed this morning that he barely knew she existed. The only reason he'd done the evil deed with her was because…well, because he'd been a hot-blooded, horny boy.

She stopped halfway to the car. The air was cool, the breeze crisp. It should have helped calm the giddy, ridiculous buzz of expectation swirling inside her head and chest.

"Focus. Focus," she softly murmured. "Don't forget he tried to rob you."

A sobering thought. Unfortunately the image of a down-and-out Eli couldn't quite overshadow the memory she'd secretly nurtured all these years of the young-sex-god Eli. How many first-meet scenarios had she imagined between them? Dozens. Maybe more. None had involved getting robbed, but most had led to the kinds of things she absolutely had no business thinking about. None. At all.

Uh-huh. Then whatcha doin' thinkin' about 'em?

She shook her head and pretended to search her

pockets for her keys, in case any of her friends were watching from the window. This was silly. She was freaking out for nothing. She knew perfectly well it was dumb—no, make that self-destructive—to hope for even a nanosecond that he'd reentered her life with an actual purpose. Whatever force or forces—fate, God, the universe—might have orchestrated this meeting, Eli obviously wasn't privy to any bigger picture. Not only had he failed to recognize her when she told him her name, he only associated her with that repugnant, misogynistic nickname. What kind of idiot would look for a sign in that?

Yo' mama's kind.

"I am *not* my mother," she muttered with an indignant huff. "What do I have to do to prove that?"

Unlike her mother, Char wasn't promiscuous. She didn't party. She'd earned her own way since high school. She'd never been married let alone tied the knot with the first fairly cute loser who came along, divorced his ass a year or two later and started the whole cycle over again.

The lone impulsive slipup in Char's past that even vaguely resembled something her mother would have done involved Eli. And then she'd chosen to act responsibly—not a claim her mother ever could have made.

Did she regret her choice? Of course, but that didn't mean it hadn't been the right thing to do.

It had been. And having Eli suddenly show up out of the blue didn't mean anything. Did it?

Her normally loquacious conscience remained atypically silent.

"Fine," she muttered. "Whatever."

She hurried along the sidewalk until she could see her car. Still there, she noted, trying desperately to ignore the fluttering sensation in her belly.

She was within two steps of the vehicle when she saw that he wasn't sleeping sitting up as she'd assumed but was intently reading something on his lap. Her heart rate spiked a heartbeat before she confirmed her worst fear.

"Oh, God, no," she cried. "My journal."

CHAPTER FOUR

ELI HEARD CHAR'S CRY of alarm but he was too numb to react. A drum was thumping inside his brain. The words she'd written in a girlish combination of print and cursive seemed burned into his mind.

Guess who took care of him? Yep, me. And by *took care* I mean what you think. Why? Because I knew I'd never get another chance. Who wouldn't make love to a god?

She'd spent two pages describing a night Eli could barely remember. His bachelor party had started out like any other party. His cousin—and then best friend—Robert had taken him out to Lake Sharpe to meet a bunch of friends and teammates. At some point in the night he and Robert had gotten into a fistfight. Eli couldn't remember what they'd been fighting about. He vividly recalled everyone freaking out.

"Holy shit, Robert," someone had shouted.

"Bobbi's gonna skin you alive if Eli shows up with two black eyes and a broken nose."

He vaguely recalled Robert helping him stumble up to the back door of the dyke nurse's house. Everyone knew her sexual preferences—even if nobody in their right mind would have openly "come out of the closet" in such a conservative and close-minded atmosphere. The truth didn't keep people in need from seeking her services. Got an itch that probably didn't come from a toilet seat? Go see the elder Jones sister. Need stitches but can't afford the E.R.? Pam Jones would help you out for a few bucks, a barter or for free, if it came right down to it.

People like Eli went to Nurse Jones when you didn't want your business spread around town. He sorta remembered knocking on her door, but not much after that. He had no memory whatsoever of what Char had written. And he wasn't sure he even believed any of it. Especially the part that showed up toward the end of the book.

I haven't written for a long time because I didn't want to take a chance on Mom or Aunt Pam finding this and reading that I was pregnant. I didn't think it could happen from just one time, but it did. Too bad Eli's happily married and living in San Diego.

Now that Pam's found out, I'm not sure

what's going to happen. Mom threw her usual hissy fit. There's talk of sending me to live with Aunt Marilyn in Montana. Like that's going to happen. I'd run away and take my chances on the street before I'd put my baby within a mile of that creepy uncle of mine. All I know is it's hard to be miserable when you're carrying Eli Robideaux's baby.

The door wrenched open. "Give me that. You had no right."

He looked at the irate woman with the weird hair. She was leaning in, her hand extended. It shook with barely concealed fury. Or fear. He didn't know. He couldn't think and that made him more pissed off than he'd been all day.

"You're a liar. This didn't happen," he cried, crushing the notebook in his fist. It felt good to yell at someone.

She yanked the book from him and pressed it to her chest. Her voluminous chest. A tiny hint of something akin to a memory flitted through his brain.

No. It didn't happen. She was a messed-up kid with a big-time crush. I wouldn't. I didn't.

"I don't lie. Get out of my car."

He looked from the notebook flattened against her pumpkin-colored sweater to her face. A stranger's face. "I'd remember if that happened.

I'm not the kind of guy who went around screwing innocent little girls."

She dropped her chin in a challenging way. "Really? That number below your name in the yearbook—twenty-three, wasn't it?—didn't match the number on your basketball jersey. I always heard it stood for the number of girls you—"

"No." He put his hand to his face and groaned. "That was a joke. Robert started that rumor. It wasn't true. Not even close. I wasn't a saint, but still…"

"You were passed out drunk when your cousin dropped you off at my aunt's back door. He basically carried you to the gurney. She was on duty at the hospital. I was going to let you sleep it off, but you woke up. We talked."

He tried to picture the scene. If he could recall what she looked like back then, maybe he could figure out what was true. But even studying her face didn't bring back anything. "What did we talk about?"

"Your situation. The fact that Bobbi was pregnant and that was why you were marrying her."

"I wouldn't have—"

She interrupted. "Everyone knew it. You weren't spilling some big secret. My friends believed she got pregnant on purpose to trap you into marrying her. I told them you were too smart for that."

"Dumb, you mean. Blind, smug and dumb. That was my dad's opinion. But the point is I was loyal. I wouldn't have done what you wrote. Not on the night before my wedding."

She took a step back. "Really? You're sure about that? You can't remember anything. You don't remember me. But you're sure."

He hated having to swallow the lump that suddenly developed in his throat before he could answer. "Yes."

"Then how do you explain what I wrote in my journal dated that night?"

"F-fantasy?"

"Why? Why would I make something like that up? On the off chance that you became president someday? Maybe I was a fifteen-year-old blackmailer? Maybe I'm crazy and this is a plot to screw with your head?"

He kicked the heel of his boot against the floorboard with such force the entire car shook. "How the hell should I know? You tell me."

She gave the notebook a shake. "I did. You read it yourself. Firsthand observation trumps vague recollection every time."

She had a point. If he weren't so messed up and his head wasn't pounding like he'd been on a three-day binge, he might have conceded round one to her, but he couldn't. That would lead to a can of worms he didn't have the energy to think about, much less let loose.

He grabbed the hood of his sweatshirt and yanked it upward. Sinking in the seat, he did his best to disappear. "I can't believe this is happening," he muttered. "Talk about going from bad to worse. If I ever get my hands on that dumb-ass uncle of mine, he's going to wish he'd never been born. 'A part of you is missing, nephew,'" he said in a singsong voice. "'The answer you seek is in *Paha Sapa.*'"

His disdain for the Black Hills couldn't have been missed.

"Was that supposed to be your impression of Joseph or Yoda?" she asked sardonically.

Her tone was less angry than it had been, but he heard a tremor of bruised feelings. He'd done something—whether intentional or not—that affected her back in high school. She'd been a kid.

So was I.

But that argument didn't hold water because he'd never really been a kid. His parents' loud and turbulent love-hate relationship, their divorce, his mother's remarriage and subsequent death from ovarian cancer when Eli was thirteen contributed to his very truncated childhood. He'd grown up too fast. People had depended on him from a very young age. His mother. His younger half siblings.

His alcoholic father. Then Bobbi, who was by far a better mother than she was wife.

What did the county shrink call him? An enabler. He'd enabled the people he loved to take advantage of his need to be needed. A character flaw that probably contributed to his decision to go into law enforcement.

"Can you take me back to the main road? If not, I can walk there." Liar. He'd probably fall flat on his face if he made it a block.

She didn't answer right away but a few seconds later he heard her sigh. "Okay. I said I'd take you to Sturgis and I will."

As she walked past the front of the car, Eli caught a glimpse of her profile and a shiver of recognition traveled from the nucleus of his brain to the tips of his boots. "Boobs Jones makes my Johnson hard" someone had scribbled on the door of the boys' can. He might have had a wet dream or two at her expense himself. He couldn't say for sure, but there was always plenty of speculation over the exact size and shape of the breasts freshman Charlene Jones kept hidden under her bulky sweatshirts.

Which, he told himself, was the main argument against her story being true. If he'd had a chance to see and/or touch Char Jones's nubile breasts, the image would have been seared into his brain—even if he was on a gurney in her aunt's kitchen with a possible concussion.

"Why would I blank out something like that?" he asked as they backtracked through town. A few of the landmarks, like the stupid little dinosaur next to the Civic Center, looked familiar thanks to the television show he'd caught a couple of time with his daughters. But at the moment he didn't gave a rat's ass about seeing it.

"How would I know?"

"Were you on top? Or was I?"

The passenger-side tire dropped into a rut on the shoulder of the road. It took her a few heart-stopping seconds to recover. Enough to make Eli's knuckles turn white from clenching his fists. "Forget I asked. Dumb question."

"You'd been in a fight. For all I knew you were suffering from a concussion. I did my best to keep you calm and stable until my aunt came."

"By jumping my bones?" he asked, reserving the right to use blunter terms later on.

"Not at first." He looked at her and saw how pink her cheeks had become. A pretty color that made her look a good twenty years younger than he felt. "I was treating your cut when my aunt called to say there was an accident on the bridge and she wouldn't be home for several hours. She wanted me to know my mother wasn't involved."

He frowned, confused.

Char took her hand off the wheel and made a wobbly motion. "Aunt Pam had a police scanner, and on the nights my mom was late coming home, Pam knew I'd sit in the kitchen listening. Mom partied a lot."

He understood. His father had lost his license twice that Eli knew of. "Did you tell your aunt I was there?"

She shook her head. "I'm not a doctor, but even I could tell that cut above your eye wasn't life threatening. I managed to close it with two little sutures and a bandage. My only real concern was whether or not you had a concussion. I figured the best thing I could do was try to keep you awake."

"And you figured the best way to do that was by having sex?"

His cynical tone made her scrunch up her face and sort of duck her head. The car wove slightly between the two lanes. "Maybe we should talk about this later."

He searched his memory again, trying to pull some image to mind that might back up her story. What did the place look like? Nothing. Was the treatment room her kitchen? He didn't think so but he couldn't say why. Was he on a gurney? He'd seen all kinds on the job. If the one he'd been on had wheels...he couldn't picture making love on the move.

"Where'd we do it?"

She shook her head, as if she'd been expecting the question. "Pam saw patients in a small room off the kitchen. It was a screened porch when my grandparents lived there. She bought a used examination table from an old clinic. The back was raised about like this." She held her hand horizontally between them then made the fingers tilt upward to a sixty-degree angle. "I thought it would be better to keep your head elevated."

He could have said something coarse but he managed to bite his tongue. "You were on top?"

"Yeah. It seemed safer—concussionwise."

He turned to look at her, but it took too much effort to keep his gaze off her chest so he slumped again and closed his eyes. "Do you really expect me to believe that a virgin would climb on top of an injured guy in her aunt's makeshift E.R. where anybody could walk in?"

He heard her take in a deep breath, but he willed his eyes to remain closed. *No leering.*

"It didn't take all that long, Eli. I put my hand down there and you were instantly hard. The smart thing would have been to give you a blow job, but I didn't know how."

His eyes popped open. "What do you mean you didn't know how? That's a no-brainer."

The car made another unscheduled jog across the middle divider as she tossed up her hands on the steering wheel. "I'm sure I could have figured it out, but at the time, I didn't want to look like a novice. Everyone said Bobbi was the best in school when it came to giving bj's, and since you were marrying her the next day…"

He groaned, wishing he'd never asked. His soon-to-be ex-wife was a topic he had no intention of discussing. "So you got naked and hopped on top of me?"

"You wish," she sputtered, tapping the brakes to round a curve in the road. "Like you said, anybody could have walked in. As it happened, when Robert brought you in, it was past midnight. I'd already changed into my nightgown."

Nightgown? A tingle of something he didn't want to acknowledge shot down his spine. He gulped loudly. "Pink flannel?"

Her shoulders lifted and fell. "I don't know. Maybe. Yeah, actually, I think it was. We had a warm spring then suddenly in early June the weather turned cold. I remember someone saying if it snowed on her wedding, Bobbi was going to make the weatherman pay."

He muttered a string of words he'd have busted his son's chops for using. He'd had a dream for years that he secretly called his guilty pedophile dream. Only now he knew it wasn't a dream, it was a memory.

Neither said anything for several miles. They

were approaching the intersection of the main highway—he knew because he could see the cross-members of her teepee—when he worked up the nerve to ask, "So you had an abortion, huh?"

"What?"

Her shriek made the hair on the back of his neck stand on end. She stomped on the brakes so hard he had to brace his hands on the dash, despite the safety belt that cut into his chest. The rebound slammed him against the seat.

The car slid sideways to a stop in the gravel driveway they'd left an hour or so earlier. "Get out. You're not the man I thought you were. Back then or now. Go. Take the money I gave you and leave. Now."

She reached across him to open the passenger door. Her body touched him—that is, her wool jacket pressed against his grubby thermal sweatshirt, which covered a couple of other layers. There was nothing sexual in the touch. Nothing sexual between them. Only anger and hurt on her part, and confusion and desperation on his. No reason in the freaking world for him to kiss her.

But he did. Hard, fast, deep, hot. And what flared to life like a fire carefully banked in a stark, barren hearth made less sense than anything that had happened so far. But, Lord God, it felt good. It felt real. Like a lifeline that would keep him from falling into the bone-deep despair that had been his father's ruin.

THE LAST THING IN THE WORLD Char had expected was for Eli to kiss her. Not a mushy Thank-God-I-finally-found-you kiss. Things like that only happened in romance novels. No. His lips were icy-cold, despite the heat blasting from the defroster. His breath was surprisingly pleasant—as if he'd just sucked on a candy cane—but his several-days-old stubble felt like tiny wires piercing her skin.

It should have been the kiss from hell.

Should have been.

Instead of freaking out—was the car completely off the road? She couldn't say for certain—she actually leaned in and made a little sighing sound that she couldn't believe came from her lips. She was embarrassed, but not enough to push him away.

Even the fury she'd initially felt when he suggested that she might have had an abortion disappeared the moment he pulled her against him. She wasn't herself. She was... *Oh, no, I've turned into my mother.*

'Cept ya aren't drunk.

No. She was stone-cold sober and she was making out with Eli Robideaux in her Honda, a stone's throw from her store, where her clerk and any customers could be watching. "This is nuts," she cried, pushing back. "I must be nuts."

Her words were more effective than the pressure she exerted against his shoulders. He stopped kissing her immediately. He was breathing hard and now she could smell a stale hint of burnt tobacco on his breath. And sage?

The musky, not completely pleasant scent helped clear her head. "You need a toothbrush," she told him. "And a shower."

He let out a gruff snort but didn't argue the point. Or apologize.

She eased her foot off the brake and drove straight to her garage. The door was up, she noticed. Not something she ever did, since one half of the space was devoted to boxes of stock and seasonal displays. She pulled into the empty slot and killed the engine.

"I'll make you a deal," she said, knowing there was no turning back from the confrontation that was coming. "I'll wash your clothes while you clean up. We can talk over a bowl of soup. After that, I'll drive you to Sturgis."

He didn't jump at the offer. "My uncle's staying with a woman I only met once a long time ago. I'm not sure I can find her place in the dark. She doesn't have a phone."

She picked up her purse and took the key out of the ignition. "I can't do anything about that. It gets dark early in the mountains." She pointed over her shoulder. "You're welcome to try your luck hitching again, but I really think we should talk about this like civilized adults. Seventeen years is a long time."

He didn't argue. He got out of the car and followed her, even hitting the button to close the garage door without being asked. She found that odd, but she didn't say anything.

There was a lot to say. Too much, in fact. She'd always assumed that eventually her day of reckoning would come. With her son, not with Eli. She never saw this coming, and now it was too late to run away.

CHAPTER FIVE

ELI STAYED IN THE SHOWER longer than he had in his entire life. For several minutes, he stood directly under the powerful stream of hot water without moving. Maybe if he stood here long enough, the blood in his brain would start flowing again and he could come up with some kind of plan. He hoped.

When the heat started to diminish, he grabbed a bottle of shampoo and lathered up. The scent was crisp and clean, faintly antiseptic. He didn't recognize the brand, but he knew it wasn't one Bobbi ever bought. For as long as he could remember he'd been using fruity-smelling girly products.

He never complained, but honestly, didn't anyone question his needs? If he happened to use the basement shower near his son's room, he found manly scented products. *How come E.J. rated,* he silently grumbled, *and I didn't?*

He now knew the answer, but he didn't want to think about it. Instead he redirected his ire toward the woman he'd been married to for almost twenty years. She did the shopping. Were her purchasing habits one more way to emasculate the man of the house?

He rinsed his hair and turned off the water. Thinking about Bobbi left a bitter taste in his mouth. He hated being angry all the time. Maybe that as much as anything had been his motivation behind falling for his uncle's vision quest baloney. He wanted to start moving forward. If that meant he needed to fill in a few gaps in his past…well, who could have known the gaps involved other human beings?

He used the big, fluffy, chocolate-colored towel that was hanging beside the shower to dry off, then he wiped the condensation from the mirror and looked at himself. Haggard. Worn down. Defeated. The way his father had looked the entire time Eli had known him.

With his hands pressed flat against the countertop on either side of the sink, he leaned heavily on his arms. For the past six months his life had been spiraling downward like a jet plane in free fall. He'd fueled the propulsion with anger and self-pity.

"Enough," he said, looking himself in the eye. "Enough."

He shaved and brushed his teeth using the disposable razor and new toothbrush Char had provided. A thick, white terry-cloth robe—the kind you could pick up at fancy hotels—was hanging from a hook behind the door. He put it on and knotted the belt at his waist.

He ran his fingers over the insignia on the breast pocket but he didn't recognize the chain. No surprise there. Other than Disney World and a few family-friendly motels between Lower Brule and Enid, Oklahoma, Eli didn't have a lot hotel experience.

Was Char a world traveler, he wondered, stuffing his hands in the side pockets?

Char. A virtual stranger with a secret connection to him he still wasn't certain he believed. And he'd kissed her. For no logical reason. Was he hoping to prompt some clear memory? Or was his action plain old lust?

Lord knew he hadn't been with a woman for months. He couldn't remember the last time he and Bobbi had made love. In hindsight, he wondered if she'd suspected what the results of E.J.'s DNA test would reveal. Maybe she'd been preparing herself—and him—by squeezing him out of her life.

He closed the lid of the toilet and sat, stalling. If what Charlene wrote was true, his life was about to change in ways he probably couldn't imagine. Another kid? A hidden child he'd never heard about? A boy child, he gathered. His *real* kid. Maybe. Unless Char was as gifted a liar as Bobbi.

He closed his eyes and rested his chin on the heel of his hand. His lips twitched as he pictured himself assuming the pose of that famous sculpture—*The Thinker.* He wasn't. Obviously. If he'd thought more and screwed around less, maybe he wouldn't be in this situation. Either of these situations.

No, Bobbi was the thinker in the family. Her animal totem was the fox, and all the standard appellations applied. She'd cleverly plotted and manipulated and got her way from that spring day their senior year of high school when she broke the news that she was pregnant.

Eli had known for a long time that she wanted him to marry her, but he'd had other plans. And even though he'd been the one to insist on always using a condom when they fooled around, she'd wound up pregnant.

"Rubbers aren't perfect, Eli," she'd told him, sobbing in a way that reminded him of his mother at the end of her life when the pain was so bad. Bobbi had even backed up the claim with some statistics she'd gotten from the health teacher.

He'd accepted what she told him at face value. Why wouldn't he? He wasn't the most egotistical guy around, but he knew girls liked him. More than a few had thrown themselves at him over the years. It never once crossed his mind that Bobbi might have been screwing some other guy at the same time. Especially Eli's cousin—and best friend—Robert.

That old infidelity might have hurt but it wouldn't have been enough to cause Eli's whole life to implode, if it hadn't been for the DNA test E.J. had asked him to take. Eli had never really understood the reason behind the test. All he knew was the end result. "We share a bunch of the same genetic markers, Dad, but there's a ninety-five percent probability you're not my father," E.J. told him.

The printout was like a W.M.D.—it blew the roof off their fairly happy home and sent the survivors spinning off in every direction. Bobbi took the girls to her parents'. E.J. moved in with a friend. Eli spent every waking hour somewhere else, unable to walk through the empty rooms without feeling consumed by anger.

He squared his shoulders. He wasn't proud of the way he handled things. Too much self-righteousness and not enough forgiveness, his grandmother would have said. Bobbi had accepted her guilt. "Yes, I slept with Robert when I was seeing you, but I was sure you were E.J.'s father. I wouldn't have married you if I didn't think so."

Eli didn't know if he believed her or not. He was pretty sure he could never trust her again. A moot point because Bobbi had decided that their marriage had become stagnant and unfulfilling. "All we do is work and dash around to the kids' activities," she'd told him as she packed their daughters' things. "The passion between us has been gone for years, Eli. Maybe you choose not to see that, but I can't pretend anymore."

Pretense. A word he hated like no other. His father had accused him of pretending to want a college career. On her deathbed, his mother admitted that she'd pretended to love his father as a way of escaping her brutal father. And his wife, who slept with another man while dating him, accused him of faking his commitment to his family.

He'd lost it. The guy who rarely argued, let alone lost his temper, blew up. His daughters were so scared they called 9-1-1. The cops who raced to his house were friends, coworkers, but they'd looked at Eli as if he were a stranger.

Bobbi and the girls moved in with her folks in Reliance. His captain ordered Eli to take six weeks of personal leave. The first two weeks, Eli spent in an alcohol-induced fog of self-pity. Then, out of the blue, Uncle Joseph showed up.

Given a little time and distance, Eli was certain he could rebuild a relationship with his daughters. Even E.J. might come around eventually. Unless some new dynamic added a fatal blow to his already tenuous hold on his family.

What Char was suggesting might be the last straw, but could he ignore the possibility? If it was true.

That was the question, wasn't it? he thought, pushing to his feet. *Did I really screw Char Jones and conveniently forgot about it for seventeen years?*

He looked in the mirror again, pulling down the skin under one eye to examine the red web of veins. He'd cleaned up his act years ago, thank God. Joining the Marines had provided a serious wake-up call. He'd coughed up green phlegm the first three days of boot camp—the result of too much senior partying after basketball season ended.

He'd kicked the habit. He didn't drink or smoke. He couldn't say the same for his extended family. Bobbi was still a bit of a party girl. Eli's father had been a full-fledged alcoholic right up to the day he died. Joseph seemed half-looped most of the time, but he still managed to drive around the state to attend ceremonies and powwows.

A light knock sounded on the door. "Eli?"

"Yeah?"

"Would you like a quesadilla with your soup?"

The immensity of his earlier hunger returned. "Sure."

"I'll be in the kitchen when you're ready. I'm setting a pair of moccasins beside the door."

"Moccasins?" he said, opening the door. "How could you have a pair my si—"

She was gone, but a shoebox answered his question. Her shop. She'd run next door and picked out a pair for him—probably using his hiking boots to determine the correct size.

Crap. He scowled at his image in the mirror one last time. He didn't deserve this kind of hospitality. And he had no idea when he'd be in a position to repay it.

He picked up the box and started to walk in the direction she'd pointed out when they first entered the home. While the hallway wasn't that chilly, gooseflesh appeared on his bare legs. Sleeping outdoors the night before had introduced a permanent chill in his bones.

He quickly returned to the bathroom and opened the box. The moccasins were a work of art. Fleece lined, the dark hide exterior was adorned with intricate beading by a truly skilled artisan. He felt guilty about knocking her store as a repository for cheap crap made in China.

He put them on and stood. Oddly they made him feel more like himself. The old Eli. The person he no longer recognized when he looked in the mirror.

But he didn't take a chance on checking his reflection to see who might be standing there. Ex-Marine? Underpaid cop whose job was hanging by a thread? Soon-to-be divorced father of three? Or four?

He walked to the kitchen quietly. The way he and Robert had practiced when they were kids. Char apparently hadn't heard his approach. She was standing over a pan, frowning at it intently.

"Didn't anyone ever tell you a watched pot never boils?"

She spun around too fast and accidentally knocked the pan's handle. To Eli's surprise, his reflexes actually responded quickly enough to keep it from falling. Some of the liquid sloshed over his hand. Hot, but not as bad as he feared.

"Oh, man." She groaned. "I'm such a klutz in the kitchen. If I didn't have friends who cook, I'd be in bad shape."

They were close enough that Eli had an unrestricted view of her shape. Aside from the odd-colored hair, she looked great. She'd lost the deep purple wool jacket. Her sweater—the same one she'd had on when he first stepped into her shop—was an eye-catching orange. The color was vivid, like her hairdo. He wondered why she no longer looked as strange as he'd first thought.

He hoped his change of heart wasn't influenced by their kiss. He might be a hardship case, but he wasn't dumb enough to get involved with someone who claimed to share a place in his history. He stepped back to put more room between them.

"Smells good," he said, licking the drop that rested on his wrist.

"I can't take credit for it," Char said, turning back to the stove. "But I am glad the canned soup industry got smart and started making stuff that's semigood for you. Still more salt than you need," she added matter-of-factly, "especially if you add crackers, but better than the crap my mother made for me."

Her complaint held only a small hint of bitterness. He tried to remember what he knew about her family. Lots had been said about the Jones sisters, but whether or not any was factual he couldn't say. Eli vaguely recalled his dad pointing out Char's grandfather at a corner table of a local watering hole one day. The only reason the memory stuck was that the old man had been chomping on a fat cigar and had a huge pile of chips in front of him. "Some assholes have all the luck," Dad had whispered. "But that doesn't make 'em a winner."

"Your grandpa was a gambler, wasn't he?"

Char shrugged. "Could be. I only knew him as the mean voice behind a curtain. Like in *The Wizard of Oz,* only grumpier."

His daughters had loved that movie when they were younger. Had he ever taken the time to watch it with them? He didn't think so. The realization made his stomach ache. It made a loud grouchy noise of its own.

"I'm hurrying," she said, directing her comment toward his middle. The fact that her gaze lingered a moment and even seemed to travel lower set off another reaction—less noisy, but more noticeable.

Worried that he might embarrass himself further, he moved to a chair at the round oak table and sat. He crossed his legs and parked his elbow on his knee. "You don't need my help, do you?"

"No. I'm not Martha Stewart, but I can heat soup without poisoning my guests." She took a hunk of pepper cheese out of the refrigerator and started grating it onto a plate. "Having you out of the way is better, in fact. I'm used to having the place to myself."

"No significant other?"

"What's that mean?" she asked, looking up from what she was doing. Her tone was noticeably testy.

"Um…I wondered whether or not to expect some guy with a 'Remember the Little Big Horn' patch on his cap to come charging through the door to protect his territory."

She relaxed visibly. "Oh." She gave the soup one more stir, then held her hand flat, an inch or so above the large skillet that was heating on the stove. "I thought you were making an allusion to my aunt's situation."

"Which aunt? Didn't you have two? The nurse and—"

"Aunt Pam was a nurse-practitioner. My aunt Marilyn was married to a holy roller who ran that little church in Fort Pierre. They eventually moved to Montana."

"More Indians to convert?"

"Less opportunity for Marilyn to escape her creep-oid husband," she said, more to herself than to him. She startled guiltily when she glanced sideways and made eye contact with him. "There are so many skeletons in the Jones's family closet we barely have room for coats."

Her wit surprised him. He didn't know why. "Yeah, well, it's a new world. Being gay isn't one of those black hole kind of secrets. Just ask my stepbrother."

"Seriously? You knew about my aunt?"

Everyone in Pierre had speculated about her aunt's sexual proclivity. "The nurse or the preacher's wife?"

Her grin told him she knew he was kidding. "The nurse."

"Does she still live in Pierre?"

"No. Hasn't for years. She lives in San Francisco with her longtime partner. A surgeon."

He was glad to hear it. "Good. She helped a lot of people through some pretty tough situations. I give her credit for that."

Char didn't reply. She seemed intent on flipping the tortilla, but it could be that he'd said something wrong. When she carried the bowl of steaming, fragrant soup to the table and placed it before him, he stopped her—one hand lightly touching her wrist. "You don't agree?"

She shook her head, the multicolored strands catching the light in an interesting way. "I've never had a problem with Pam's sexual orientation. She provided some stability when my mom was strung out or too in love to remember she was a mother. But she could be very opinionated, and she expected people to do what she said without argument—especially members of her family."

The last proviso seemed to hold significance. Eli watched her dash back to the stove. A minute or so later, she delivered a plate with a golden browned tortilla that she'd cut into eight triangular pieces.

She returned to the counter for a pair of ceramic salt and pepper shakers shaped like turkeys. She set them on the table near his bowl. "When Pam found out about me, she immediately made a plan. Well…um…after she gave me a physical and determined it was too late for me to safely—or legally—have an abortion." She stumbled over the word. Eli bet it constantly tripped her, even after all these years.

He had a lot of questions, but the aroma of the soup was making his mouth water too badly to get a word out. He picked up the spoon she'd already set on top of a pretty green and black linen napkin and dug in.

She scuttled back to the counter and returned a second later with a glass of milk. Milk. Something his mother would have done. Bobbi, who was lactose intolerant, only bought milk for the children. She yelled at him if she ever saw him take a swig.

"I'll let you eat in peace. Your clothes are probably ready to go into the dryer."

Good, he thought, tearing off a hunk of cheese and tortilla to dunk in the bowl. Hell, the last time he tried to cook for himself, he'd nearly burned down the place. Bobbi had won blue ribbons for her pies and breads at various fairs, but her menu planning changed dramatically when she took a job at the casino three years earlier.

The money had come in handy—E.J. needed braces, Micah was asthmatic and Juline was a clotheshorse. Looking back, Eli wondered exactly when he went from daddy to Daddy Warbucks.

Lately it seemed as though he was the guy who said no all the time.

I sucked as a parent.

"Really? I figured you'd be a great dad."

He nearly choked on the swallow of soup that was halfway down his throat. He hadn't realized he'd voiced the thought out loud.

"What are you—a mind reader? Do those funny streaks of color hide your antennae?"

She laughed and wiggled her index fingers upward through her hair. "Like in *My Favorite Martian?* I used to watch reruns on Friday night. While you were making the All-State Boys' Basketball team."

"For all the good it did me," he muttered under his breath. He knew she was close enough to hear, so he quickly asked, "How come you weren't at the games?"

"I was. Sometimes. If Mom was seeing somebody halfway decent. But when she was alone… well, weekends were tricky. Sobriety-wise, Fridays were the worst day of the week."

He didn't need her to explain. His father had only remained sober during basketball season because he had such high hopes for Eli. Once those hopes were squashed, Dad went back to his usual pattern: work, drink, tear down everything you spent the week building, pass out, promise to do better, work, drink…et cetera, et cetera.

Neither spoke for a few minutes, then Char straightened and folded her hands on the table in front of her. He studied her hands. Short nails. No polish. Three, handcrafted rings—two with stones, one plain. All pretty and delicate on her strong, resourceful-looking fingers.

"I suppose I should fill in the blanks about what happened," she said. "That journal you were reading ended with me admitting I was pregnant.

What came next…" Her voice trailed off a moment, then she added, faking a smile, "Is in another book. Black cover. For obvious reasons."

He wiped his mouth with the napkin and pushed the bowl aside. Easing back against the chair, he said, "Okay. Tell me what happened. But make it the truth. I'm a cop. I can tell when someone's lying." He wished. He'd never once suspected his wife had been keeping a life-altering secret from him all these years.

"I told you before," she said stiffly, her small, pointed chin lifting. "I don't lie."

Their gazes met and held. He believed her. "Go on."

"You read the passage about what happened the night you came to my aunt's. I didn't plan it. Obviously."

He believed that. "You acted on impulse. I get that. What I don't get is why?"

"I was fifteen. Kids that age do dumb things without thinking about the repercussions."

Fifteen. Micah was fifteen. "Why me?"

"I had a crush on you. I don't know why, but I sorta built up this fantasy about you and me. If you read any of my earlier diaries, you'd see your name mentioned quite often. So when you showed up out of the blue that night… Well, I guess you could say I took advantage of you."

He hadn't heard anyone use that phrase in a

long time. His ego wasn't wild about the idea that anyone could have used him, although that summed up what Bobbi did.

"It was a dumb thing to do, I know," she said. "But…" She took a breath and slowly let it out. His gaze was drawn to her chest.

Damn. He'd held those breasts in his hands and didn't remember? What the hell was wrong with him?

She pounded her fist on the table to get his attention. Eli was ashamed but he wasn't going to apologize. "I'm trying to remember."

"Well, don't. It wasn't that great. You were drunk. I was a virgin. It was over…fast. And you took off when I got up to go to the bathroom. Some bloody bandages were all that was left behind. I burned those in the incinerator behind the house and never told anyone what happened between us."

He wondered if she burned the sheet, too. Had it contained a smear of her virgin blood? A sadness he didn't want to feel passed over him.

"I read about your wedding in the paper. They described the whole thing. Right down to the kind of flower in the lapel of your tux." Which she'd cut out and pasted into her journal. He'd seen the yellowed clipping. Bobbi had one just like it in their wedding album.

"A few weeks later I heard you joined the Marines."

He nodded. "Seemed like the smart thing to do for a guy with a high school diploma and a kid on the way." He didn't try to soften the snarl that came from describing that turning point in his life.

"I told myself I was happy for you," she said. "I got something from you—more than I expected as I later found out, but at the time I was satisfied."

He wondered if he'd given her any satisfaction that night. She'd implied not, but he hadn't been a complete novice when it came to pleasing women. He might have asked if the question wouldn't have come off sounding completely lame and a dozen and a half years too late.

"When did you find out you were pregnant?" There, he could be a grown-up.

She looked reflective. "I think I knew within a couple of weeks. Not possible, I've been told. But I knew. Deep down. The old bla—" She caught herself from saying something she didn't want him to hear. Another secret? "A voice in my head told me I was pregnant, but I refused to believe her. It, I mean."

He tried to picture Char coping with such a scary reality, alone. Micah's age. A tenth-grade student with her whole life ahead of her—and a new life inside her. "You must have been scared."

She shook her head. "One would think, right?

But actually, I was happy. Excited. Delirious. That's why I kept it a secret for as long as I could. I knew that once everyone else found out—my mother and Pam, in particular—there'd be holy hell to pay. So as long as it was just me and the baby I could be as happy as I wanted to be."

As happy as I wanted to be. The words sounded eerily familiar, but Eli couldn't place them.

"That's not the kind of thing you can keep secret forever."

"I know. Eventually the school called my mother because I'd been skipping P.E. It wasn't like I had any choice after a certain point. If I'd showered with the other girls I would have been outed immediately. I got by longer than I expected by stealing my aunt's prescription pad and writing an excuse of contagious impetigo. I didn't know what that was, but it sounded bad, and nobody seemed in a rush for me to share water or towels with my classmates."

"Eventually someone complained?"

"Miss Duty. Can you believe we had a P.E. teacher named Duty? Only in Pierre."

Eli remembered the woman all too well. She'd come on to him—in a broadly flirtatious way—after practice one day. He could have nailed her without a backward glance…if he hadn't been on-again with Bobbi at the time. "And…"

"She called my aunt. I always wondered if

Miss Duty was secretly gay." She paused a moment as if to reconsider the possibility. Eli kept his opinion to himself. "Anyway, Aunt Pam went ballistic. She looked at me—really looked at me—and instantly guessed what was going on. It got loud and ugly around my house for about a week, until I finally confessed what happened."

"You told them you had unprotected sex with an Indian. I bet that went over well."

She looked miffed. "Your ethnicity wasn't mentioned. In fact, your name didn't come up until I filled out the birth certificate. Naturally there was some speculation about the baby's heritage after he came out because he had a full head of glossy black hair." She paused as if tripping over that specific memory was painful. "But my hair's pretty dark without the high-lights."

"So my name is on the kid's birth certificate." Not that that proved anything. His name was on E.J.'s, too.

Char didn't answer right away. "No," she finally said.

"No?"

"Pam totally went off when she saw your name. She said the last thing any of them needed was for some tribal muck-a-mucks to get involved. She balled up the form and threw it in the garbage. She came back a few minutes later with another blank one and made me put *unknown* on the line where the father's name is supposed to go. She said no one would question it because I was my mother's daughter."

The way she said the last told him more than he wanted to know. He felt an unwelcome tug of sympathy. "Emotional blackmail," he said softly.

Her pretty eyes were tear-free. "It worked. I knew in an instant I didn't want my kid to have the kind of family life I had. The kind of family life he would have had if he'd stayed with me." She looked at him, chin high. "Pam arranged for a private adoption. I didn't see the family, but they met my criteria."

"What kind of criteria?"

"I…" She looked down. Was this when the lies started? "At least one of the parents had to be Native American. I wanted our son to be proud of his heritage."

Eli couldn't repress his scorn for her naiveté. "Wherever he is, I'm sure he thanks you a lot for that."

She sat forward. "What do you mean?"

"Oh, come on, Char. You grew up in South Dakota. You know what happens to kids on the *rez.*" He used the slang he heard every day on the job. "Even the best and the brightest somehow get sucked into the vortex. They check their ambition at the door and fall into the same old patterns of alcohol abuse and apathy."

Her face was contorted with concern. "But how could knowing about your heritage be a bad thing? You spent your summers on the reservation. You're a success story."

His laugh was anything but funny. "Right. The guy who tried to rob you. Whose career is probably dust. Whose wife left him and kids think he's the biggest jerk on the planet." Her expression turned intense as the reality of his situation sank in. "Yeah. Your kid is really going to thank you for that."

She licked her lips and swallowed. Her hands were clenched on the table, as if in prayer. "I wanted him to be proud of who he is. My family tree flattens out after two generations. Nobody remembers my great-grandparents' names or birthplace. We're a freaking bonsai. But you have this rich, beautiful culture that makes you unique and special. He should know that."

Her passionate tone and adamant conviction confused him. He didn't like being confused—the constant emotional state of his life lately. "Right. Well, he's probably a junior in high school at this point. That was a turning point in my life," he admitted. "It's the year I met Bobbi. With any luck your kid is smarter than I was."

Her clenched fists remained clenched. "Kids are smarter these days, aren't they?"

He thought about E.J., who had appeared to have his head on straight and his goals firmly in sight…until the rug was yanked out from under him. Now, according to Bobbi, his son was living with his skanky girlfriend—her words—and smoking pot every day. "Not really," he said, feeling old and tired.

Char stood. "I have the adoption papers in my safe. I haven't looked at them for years. Maybe we should try to find him. To make sure he's okay. Give him options he didn't know he had."

Options? He'd had options. Fat lot of good they'd done him. His life was too messed up at the moment to devote thought to another big unknown. Besides, he was pretty sure finding a child given up in a private adoption wasn't all that simple.

"I'm not judging you, but I am curious. How come your mom or your other aunt didn't offer to help raise the kid?"

Her elaborate shudder told him a lot. "My uncle was worse than any of my mother's boy-friends. The fact that he calls himself a man of God is such an outrage, even a dumb kid like me could see through him. Marilyn is like my grandma. Saintly martyr? Or victim of abuse? The answer depends on who you ask."

He understood. He'd seen the same scenario time and again on the job.

"As for my mother…" She let out a soft sigh. "She passed away a few years ago in Phoenix. Complications from Valley Fever. Too many vices, too many years of abusing her health. She was married to husband number four at the time. The best in a long string of losers. He was the reason she had a small estate to pass on to me," she said, gesturing toward the business he'd been in earlier. "It helped with the down payment on this place."

"What about your dad?"

"Died in a car accident when I was nine. He and Mom were divorced at the time. We moved back to Pierre when Grandpa got sick. Colon cancer," she added.

Her childhood didn't sound much happier than his, although he did have great memories of spending his summers on the reservation with his grandparents. His dad was rarely around, but Unci and Lala had been the two most special people in the world. He'd been surrounded by cousins—and kids the family took in and called cousins—and interesting adults who seemed to laugh a lot. At least, in his memories.

"Listen," he said, repressing a yawn. "This is probably a lot to ask—especially after I tried to rob you…" Her smile made him forget what he was about to say. She was beautiful. Strong features that fit her face and seemed tempered by life. In a good way—even given what he knew about that life.

"Let's agree that you weren't really a danger to me or others. A B.B. pistol can't hurt you if you don't take the safety off. So what do you want to ask me?"

"I wonder if I could bunk here tonight. The couch. Even the floor would be a big improvement over where I slept last night. I don't think I have the energy to wander around Sturgis trying to find my uncle tonight."

"Or the right jacket," she added. "You could have died of exposure, you know."

He shook his head. "I had a sleeping bag, although it was only a three-season one. Barely adequate for the temperature. And to make things worse, at some point in the night I rolled down an embankment and ripped a big hole in it. I tossed the thing in the first garbage can I came to."

"Oh. Well, it probably wouldn't have done you much good tonight. I heard it's supposed to snow."

"Great." His options were shrinking by the dozen. He'd probably have to call Bobbi in the morning to ask her to come pick him up. Lucky him.

"Of course, you can stay here. I have a guest room. My only regular visitor to use it is named Jordie."

A guy. "You're not expecting him tonight?"

She seemed amused by the question. "No. I saw him at the party today." She consulted her watch. "He's probably home in bed with a tummy ache after eating too much cake and ice cream. He's seven."

"Oh."

"He's my friend Kat's son. She lends him to me when I need a kid fix. Something I didn't even know I was missing in my life until she asked me to babysit one day. Heck, she had to twist my arm to do it. That was a few months back. Now I can't get enough. Little boys are fascinating creatures."

He pictured E.J. as a child. They'd done so much together over the years. Less once puberty hit, but from age five to twelve E.J. and Eli had been best buddies.

"Do you have any aspirin? I've got a blinding headache."

She looked at him a moment as if she might say something, but instead, she nodded and made a follow-me motion. "You can name your poison. I have every OTC drug and herbal potion known to man. I blame my aunt for this fascination I have with long, unpronounceable names for products that I usually throw out unopened when their expiration date comes up."

He couldn't imagine wasting money like that

but he didn't say so. Maybe his first impression was right after all. She was weird.

But she was offering him a warm bed, and he was willing to overlook her oddness—and the silent elephant hanging in mid-air between them—out of pure and simple exhaustion. "Thanks," he said, meaning it.

"You're welcome. No Lakota I've ever met would turn away a weary traveler."

He kept his snide comment to himself. But as he followed her down the narrow hallway, he found himself thinking that the only thing better than a warm bed might be one with a warm body in it. Hers.

He shook his head, hoping to clear away the lingering effects of his uncle's narcotics. That had to explain the irrational reaction he experienced when he was close to her. Good Lord, he had enough troubles without complicating things even more.

"Do any of those pills have a sleep aid in them?"

Her laugh was light and chirpy, like a birdcall he once heard. "That's my favorite kind. I never use them because I hate waking up groggy in the morning, but I'm a sucker for a good sleep aid ad. Dreams are not necessarily our friends."

At last. Something they both agreed upon emphatically.

CHAPTER SIX

CHAR DIDN'T EXPECT to sleep—not with Eli Robideaux in her guest room. She even pilfered two pale blue pills from the bottle she'd given him in case she tossed and turned for hours. Reliving the worst moment in her life was bad enough, but second-guessing her decision and all the hopes she'd had for her child's future was even worse. But as she closed her eyes she'd found her attention drawn in a different direction.

The moment her head hit the pillow she relived in surprising detail the kiss they'd shared that afternoon. When she rubbed her cheek on the fine thread count pillowcase, she was sorry the fabric wasn't rougher to mimic the sensation of his beard against her skin.

She didn't know why he kissed her. And her usually outspoken subconscious was remaining uncharacteristically mum on the subject. But ruminating on the possibilities seemed to relax her and within moments she was sound asleep.

"What's that about?" she asked her reflection the

next morning as she brushed her teeth. "Eli Robideaux's kiss is the cure to insomnia? Who knew?"

The words came out muffled and unintelligible, thanks to the toothbrush, but normally she didn't even have to think something to receive a lecture from the old black woman.

Today…nothing.

Not even a "Don't you dare, chickadee!" just before dawn, when Char woke up breathing hard from her dream. She'd tingled in places that hadn't seen action in months. For a minute she'd considered faking some kind of sleep disorder to accidentally-on-purpose wind up in his bed.

Her fantasies stopped the instant she tried to picture herself explaining the situation to her book club friends. They'd already heard Kat describe a bizarre Old West scenario that happened between her and Jack. Char didn't think they'd buy her sudden-onset sleepwalking excuse.

She used a hand towel to wipe away the foggy condensation on the mirror. She stared into her eyes a moment. "Stonewalling, huh? That's new." Apparently her subconscious had adopted a wait-and-see policy.

She scrunched up her nose and stuck out her tongue at the face in the mirror. Leaning close, she frowned. Was that a zit starting on her chin? *No. Please, not now.*

Before she could attack the tiny, mostly non-existent blemish, the phone rang. She gave her image one last look before dashing into the adjoining bedroom. "Hello?"

"Oh, good. You're alive. I called to make sure your mysterious old friend didn't turn out to be a serial killer."

Libby. Char glanced at the clock radio. *What took you so long?* She'd half expected her friends to start calling last night to check on her.

She pushed the speakerphone button so she could move around as they spoke. "I'm still alive and well," she said, returning the portable unit to its cradle. "Thanks for asking. How was the rest of the party?"

She tossed her towel into the bathroom then slid open the closet doors. She knew all too well she had enough clothes for three closets crammed into one tiny space. As a bit of a pack rat, she was loath to get rid of anything.

"Fabulous. Everyone had a great time. Megan was in hog heaven. The balloons were a big hit and her Tinker Bell necklace was gorgeous. Really, Char, you're too generous with all the kids. Tag's still talking about the high-tech walkie-talkies you got him for his birthday."

Char tossed a couple of layers over her shoulder to land on the bed then walked to the dresser to get her underwear. "Are you saying the necklace was too much? Too old for her?"

She slipped on her prettiest panties. For no reason other than today was…Sunday? "Is today Sunday?" she asked before Libby could answer her first question.

"Yes. Do you want to come for coffee? Coop and I are relaxing by the fire. Have you seen the snowplow go by yet?"

"Snowplow?"

Libby let out a little yip and said to someone other than Char, "She's still in bed. Char, honey, are you okay? You never sleep in."

Char leaned over to arrange her bosom in the lacy bra that she'd ordered from a catalog specializing in lingerie for the well-endowed. "Lib, nine o'clock isn't exactly sleeping in. And, if you can't tell from the noise, I'm up and at 'em. I just haven't looked outside yet."

"Oh. Well, to answer your question, Megan's gift was very special and she knows that. Mac put the necklace in a jewelry box that was her mother's, and until she's older, Megan will only wear it for special occasions…like when he and Morgan get married." The last came on a girlish squeal.

Char knew Lib was happy for her brother—especially after the recent loss of Libby and Mac's grandmother. "Have they set a date?"

"No. First, we get Kat hitched then we can work on Mac and Morgan."

Char wondered if she'd even made the edge of Libby's peripheral, happily-ever-after vision. Hard to live happily ever after alone.

"So what happened with the guy in your car?"

Char smiled as she reached for her black turtleneck. Oh, yeah, she was in Libby's headlights. "He's still here," Char said, trying to keep her voice as offhand as possible. "I gave him a shower and a hot meal, and then put him in the extra bedroom," she explained, emphasizing the last.

Silence.

She sat on the bed to pull on her silky long johns followed by jeans. Normally she would have dressed up more on a Sunday, but if it was snowing hard enough to require plows, she probably wouldn't get much business. Might as well be comfy and warm, she figured.

"Lib? Are you there?"

"Um…yeah. I'm just processing the fact that you took in a scruffy drifter off the street and let him stay at your house. That's not like you, Char. You're the smart and savvy skeptic of the book club, remember?"

And I gave him one of my best pairs of moccasins. "Eli isn't drifting. He's on a vision quest. I already told you that."

"Are you part of the vision?"

Libby was quick. And intuitive. Char didn't want to give away anything until after she and Eli had talked. In the shower, she'd come up with a plan she intended to run by him over breakfast. If he agreed to it, she was going to need Libby's help.

"He was pretty wiped out last night. We didn't talk much. If the road's open, I'll probably give him a lift to his uncle's place in Sturgis. *If* I can get Pia to come in. I didn't talk to her last night."

"You let her close without double-checking everything? Wow. This guy really does have some swoo over you."

Char ignored the comment. "How bad is this storm supposed to get? Should I even bother opening?"

They talked weather for a few minutes longer, as Char put the finishing touches on her outfit. Jewelry—her personal addiction—came last. Three silver necklaces. A wide, pounded silver bracelet from a Santa Fe artist. And last, her favorite turquoise ring.

Finally Char told Libby goodbye and walked to the bedside table to push the off button on the unit. That was when it struck her that she so rarely had guests she truly had no idea how well sound carried through the walls. When you were used to living alone, noise was not an issue.

Now you ask.

Char applied a moisturizing lip gloss that didn't require her to look in the mirror then she opened the door of her bedroom and marched down the hall. If he heard, he heard. More than likely, he was still sound asleep.

"Hey."

Or not.

She missed a step as she entered the combination kitchen and dining room. He was standing near the window. Same clothes as yesterday, of course, but clean. And he was wearing the moccasins she'd given him.

"Good morning. I thought you'd probably sleep in."

He looked at her in a guy way—not a cop way—his gaze lingering on her squash blossom necklace. Or her breasts. For once, she hoped it was the latter. She liked her body a lot better now than she had as a teen. Men liked her body, too. Sometimes that was okay…depending on the man.

"The sound of snow woke me. Thank you for not making me sleep outside last night. That would not have been fun."

"You're welcome." She paused to turn up the thermostat then she walked to the sink. She twirled the wand of the miniblinds. The whitish-gray sky seemed to absorb the outline of the teepee. Even the dark green roof of the cabin was buried under a couple of inches of fluffy white snow. "Wow. We've got ourselves a storm."

She reached for the handle of her coffeemaker's thermal carafe. "Coffee?"

"Sure. Thanks. A quick cup and I'll get out of your hair."

Self-consciously, her fingers brushed back a still-damp lock. She'd finally found a hairstylist who understood that the right cut could save hours of wasted time. "Your hair has a life of its own. You need to respect that and work with it," she'd explained to Char. "Stop trying to make it be something it isn't."

That simple credo had become a turning point for Char in several aspects of her life. She'd added the money in her breast-reduction-surgery fund to the inheritance from her mother and bought a business. She'd quit her government job and moved to the Black Hills, where she found new friends and a fresh start—with hair she still colored, but no longer tortured.

"I suppose you're wondering about the highlights, huh?" She kept her focus on the task at hand. "They were bright orange last week. For Halloween."

From the freezer, she grabbed the bag of Kona blend she bought online. "For years I went to the same hairdresser. She used a technique she called 'glitzing.' I don't know what it was, but my hair looked okay. Nothing out of the ordinary, but okay. Then Margie moved and the girl who took her place was straight out of beauty school."

She shook a domed mountain of aromatic grounds into the filter then pushed the brew button. Turning to rest the small of her back against the counter, she finished her story. "The first time she tried to duplicate Margie's color, my hair wound up looking like Little Orphan Annie meets Pink." She shrugged. "It was wild. We both cried. But she didn't dare do a reverse color for fear all my hair would fall out. I had to live with it for a few weeks, and do you know what I discovered? When you're in the business of selling things, it pays to stand out."

She glanced over her shoulder when the first hiss of dripping coffee hit the carafe. "Since then I've found that I like being different. I change the color to suit my whims and moods. It's rather liberating."

Eli had a bemused look on his face. She had the impression he didn't give a flying fig but was too polite to say so.

She spun back around. "Cereal or eggs?"

"Coffee will be fine." He barely got the word out before a deep, punishing cough intruded. He put one hand to his chest and leaned over. Char filled a glass of water and hurried to his side.

"Here. Maybe you should go back to bed. I have a vaporizer I could set up on the nightstand. And several kinds of cough syrup."

He accepted the glass and took a drink but waved aside her other suggestions. "I'm okay," he muttered.

"You need a sweat lodge."

"No, thanks. That's what got me into this mess." He gave her a flinty look. "What's with your fixation on all things Indian? Is this your way of trying to make up for what you did with me?"

She backed up in a hurry, nearly tripping over her feet. She hadn't been expecting such a sudden and unprovoked attack. "I like the heat," she said, her brain stumbling over the shattered peace she'd hoped to build between them.

"Well, I like the truth," he said after taking a gulp of water. "Comes with the job."

His tone wasn't as forceful and sincere as she'd have expected from a police officer. She wondered about the catalyst that had motivated the journey he now found himself on. "I told you the truth last night," she said. "I don't know what else you want from me, but I have something I want from you. Can we talk about it over coffee?"

He didn't answer but he did pull out a chair and plunk down heavily.

"Exactly the reason I don't take sleep aids," she

murmured, taking two large, Sioux pottery mugs from the cupboard. When she turned around, she caught the barest glimpse of a smile before his frown returned.

"Cream and sugar?" she asked, setting one of the cups in front of him.

His glossy black hair danced momentarily in the light from the window. Thick, beautiful hair. Board straight but cut to lie nicely when it was clean and combed.

She hurried to bring him a spoon, the sugar bowl and a little cardboard container of cream that she took from the refrigerator. Finally she sat across from him.

She stirred her coffee and debated about how to broach her question. "You said the reason your uncle set you on a vision que—" He started to correct her, but she stopped him. "I know. That's not the right terminology. I've tried to learn the Lakota language, but I seem to have a mental block."

Eli could sympathize. He was the same. But he didn't plan to tell her that. He'd slept well thanks to the pills he took, but in the early morning she'd come to him in his dream. He'd been sitting on a rock beside a fast-moving river. The water looked so cool and inviting he was tempted to jump in— even if it meant certain death. Then she appeared, smiling in that anything-is-possible way of hers.

She fed him sun-warmed berries from nearby bushes then they made love in the soft grass near the water's edge. At the exact moment of climax they'd both turned into birds, soaring high above the plains tableau, which to his surprise was now covered in snow. The river was gone, and he was forever changed.

He'd awoken choked up and turned on. Who needed that kind of emotional turmoil? His life was crazy enough without bird metaphors and thoughts of suicide.

"Joseph was messing with my head. I plan to find out with what when I see him. Does your car have snow tires?"

"Yes, but I'm not taking you anywhere until we talk about this. What if Joseph was right? What if the reason you're here is to find the missing piece? Correct me if I'm wrong, but wouldn't a child you didn't know about qualify?"

"Alleged child," he said, mostly out of habit. He stirred a heaping teaspoon of sugar into the aromatic black liquid then picked up the cup. His mouth started to water, but before he could take a sip, he looked across the table. Her anger was obvious in the squint of her eyes.

"Are you a cop or a lawyer? Do you want to see the alleged child's birth certificate?"

"Yes."

Her frown intensified but after a moment she

eased back in her chair. "Fine. Drink your coffee. It's in my safe in the shop. I don't open until noon on Sundays in the winter. And if this snow doesn't let up, I might not open at all," she added, looking out the window past his right shoulder.

Eli turned his chin. When he'd looked outside earlier, he'd felt a strange sort of peace. He liked the grouping of pine trees that formed a kind of sheltering cove around her little home. Another inch of the wet white stuff had fallen while they had talked.

He didn't begrudge the moisture. The entire state needed it, but he wasn't thrilled about setting out in search of his uncle in this kind of weather. Maybe he was better off calling someone else to ask for help.

But as his mind ran through the list of possible names, the emptiness in his belly became more pronounced. He hadn't made it easy for his friends and family to be supportive the past few months. The bridges were probably still there, but they were mined with sympathy. He didn't want to give people any more reason to feel sorry for him.

Maybe that had been the reason he wound up with Joseph. For all his faults, Joe spoke the truth. He didn't try to gloss over the ugly parts to make Eli feel better. "If the way was easy, people would complain about that, too," Joseph had said over their first six-pack. Their first of many.

As if tapping into his thoughts, she said, "I met your uncle at a powwow near Bear Butte a few months ago. He asked about my aunt. Small world, huh?"

Eli set down his cup a bit more forcefully than necessary. He knew what she was implying and he refused to believe it. "You think I'm here because my uncle—mystic seer that he is—found out where you lived and figured I'd unerringly stumble across you and you'd share the deep dark secret of your life with only a stolen B.B. pistol at your temple."

She not only laughed, she pretended to clap. "Now, that's more like the Eli I remember. Smart, funny, irreverent, full of himself."

"How could you know me? Except for that one night—"

"Alleged night," she put in.

He gave her a look that would have made his daughters sit back and listen.

It didn't work with her. She made a face and said, "I knew you better than you could have imagined. It's one of the unrated aspects of being invisible."

He got up and walked to the counter to refill his cup. "You were younger than me. I didn't know any underclassmen—unless they were on the basketball team or related to someone on the basketball team."

She nodded. "I'm not accusing you of ignoring me. Heck, no. I went out of my way to be invisible. You would, too, if the only thing that set you apart from the rest of the world was a pair of giant upright udders."

He bit his lip to keep from smiling. "There wasn't a single guy on the team that would have called them that."

He could tell the topic embarrassed her, but she'd been the one to bring up the subject.

"Well, maybe girls today are more comfortable with their sexuality, but my mom made such a big deal out of my figure—like I was trying to outdo her on purpose—that I did my best to be inconspicuous."

He could be thankful that at least Bobbi was a good mother. When she first told him she was leaving, he'd wanted the girls to stay with him. They'd looked at him like he was crazy. Another killer blow to his ego coming on top of learning his son wasn't his biological offspring.

He was about to bring up the subject of their supposed kid, when she said, "I signed up for every after-school activity where you might be. I took tickets at games, sold popcorn and candy at the school store, and worked in the library because you sometimes studied there."

He let out a gruff hoot. "I made out with Bobbi in the stacks, you mean. I didn't have to study that hard because I knew I was getting a basketball scholarship." He'd had one, too. For a week. "You sound like a stalker."

"I was a listener. I heard things. I knew Bobbi planned to snag you before you could get away by going to college. Although, in all fairness, I think her goal was to go with you, not to make you give up school altogether."

Bobbi. His wife's name didn't sound right coming from this stranger's lips. And yet Char wasn't a stranger. She knew more about him than he thought possible. And it made him curious. "What else do you know?"

She got up to refill her mug. He could have offered to do that for her, but this way brought her closer to him. Standing shoulder to shoulder, he could smell her light, citrus fragrance. When she leaned over to retrieve the creamer, he caught a wonderfully evocative glimpse of her breasts— even though they were completely covered all the way to her chin. Still, the outline was sexy. Black was sexy. Funny how he already knew she didn't think of herself that way. At all.

"Well…" she said, closing the fridge. "I knew that your cousin, Robert, and Bobbi—people with the same first name should never get together, don't you agree?—had a thing going before you broke up with Jenny Reid. She was a nice girl. A lot friendlier to the less popular kids

than Bobbi was. But I've observed that sometimes nice isn't as exciting as naughty. That was
certainly the case with my mom."

Eli hadn't thought of Jenny in years. "Jenny's
parents didn't like me."

"Why?"

He shrugged. "They were white. My dad was
the groundskeeper at the State House."

"You think they were prejudiced?"

He couldn't explain something as complicated
as race relations to a woman like her. But she
appeared so scandalized, he tried anyway. "They
were nice to my face, but I always felt as though
they were relieved when I left. Especially after a
quick count of the silver."

Her jaw dropped. "Did you discuss this with
Jenny?"

He shook his head. "It was easier to date
Bobbi. Her mom's Lakota. Her grandmother was
Nell Thompson. Did you ever meet her?"

She took a box of instant oatmeal—the variety
pack of flavors, he saw—from the cupboard. She
looked at him and said, "I get jittery if I drink
coffee without eating something."

He wasn't sure he believed her, but he got out
of her way and returned to the table. After she set
a kettle of water to boil, she answered his
question. "Yes, I remember Nell. I was sorry to
hear of her passing."

"I'm glad she's gone," he said, without really meaning to. "She never would have understood any of this."

She tilted her head to one side and fiddled with the long, silver and turquoise earring. The design looked complicated and expensive. For someone living in a mobile home—even a nicely finished double-wide on a permanent foundation—she seemed to have expensive tastes in jewelry.

"What else did you observe about me?" he asked, both curious and anxious to fill the silence between them.

"Well, you got better grades than anyone else on either the football team or the basketball team. Several of the track guys had 4.0s, but you were pretty smart for a jock."

"Not really. Look where I wound up."

She gave him a scolding look that reminded him of his mother. He wondered how it was possible to miss someone who had been dead for half his life.

"I do a lot of business with members of your tribe, Eli," she said. "Mostly by phone or over the Internet," she added, as if anticipating his question. *How come I've never seen you in Lower Brule?*

"From what I've heard, you're a good cop. Serious. Conscientious. Forward-thinking. My friend Linda Thompson said your son was involved in ritual dancing thanks to you."

Eli didn't dance. He would have felt like an imposter. But he had tremendous respect for the art and passion of traditional Lakota dances. He'd gotten into the project as a way to connect with E.J., who had a bit of the performer in him. Bobbi's contribution, he'd always assumed. Now he wondered if that came from Robert's side of the family.

"Yeah, well, that's in the past. My s...so—" The word wouldn't come out. "E.J. quit dancing. The only ritual I've been involved with was courtesy of my uncle, whose brain has probably become pickled from all the booze he's imbibed over the years."

The whistle from the kettle made her turn to the stove, but over her shoulder, she said, "And yet you chose him as your spiritual advisor."

Her soft snicker made him smile. Even though he was still pissed off about his circumstances, he could appreciate the irony. But he quickly reverted to his impassive cop face when she brought him his bowl of hot cereal. Surly helped keep her at a distance, which was the smart thing to do. She was pretty, kind, smart and forgiving. And he was attracted to her. Too attracted.

They ate in silence. He wolfed his down in five or six bites, the way E.J. would have. He didn't know where he left his manners—in the Badlands, maybe?

"So. Your first point was my uncle's supposed insight into my fractured psyche. What's number two?" he asked, pushing his bowl to the middle of the table.

Her hand stopped halfway to her mouth. She lowered the spoon and took a deep breath before answering. "Last night you said that seventeen was a pivotal age for you. I bet you've arrested your share of kids who made some dumb mistake at that age and spent the rest of their life regretting it."

If they had the rest of their lives. Too many wound up dead. Not that he'd tell her that. Still, the idea that any kid of his—even one he'd never heard about until yesterday—was in trouble made his breakfast lodge in his throat. "What do you expect me to do?" he asked, after swallowing a big gulp of coffee.

"I don't *expect* you to do anything, but I *want* you to help me find our son." She pushed her bowl to one side and sat forward. "I need to do this, Eli. The more time I have to think about it the more convinced I am that you're here for a reason. I can't explain why. I'm not usually a mystic, woo-woo kind of person, but your showing up at this moment in time…" She hesitated as though she might elaborate, but instead she said, "I started a college fund for him with my first paycheck. When I worked for the B.I.A., I had an automatic withdrawal that put a share of every check in his account. It's not a fortune, but I want him to have it."

"He's still a minor. You can't hand a kid money without his parents' approval."

"I know that. I wasn't suggesting we track him down and suddenly thrust ourselves into his life. Would I like to meet him someday? Of course. But that's got to be his decision. All I want for now is to know he's okay."

Eli started a mental list of all the ways a teenage boy could mess up his life. Drugs. Gangs. Reckless driving. Unsafe sex with a predatory she-bitch who screwed your best friend first. "He could be happy and safe and perfectly content. He might not even know he was adopted."

She nodded. "That's what I've prayed for every night since he was born. And if that's the case, then we're both free and clear to move on with our lives. Right?"

"Where have I heard that before?" he muttered. "Oh, yeah, Bobbi. Her parting words after she asked me for a divorce."

Char didn't say anything right away. "I'm sorry things didn't work out for you, Eli, but if you were still happily married you wouldn't have been on a vision quest. Maybe you need to find him, too. For reasons of your own."

Reasons of his own. Like to replace the son he

lost? As if that was possible. Or because this kid might be the only son he'd ever have?

"How are we supposed to find him? Didn't you say you've been looking for years?"

"I tried contacting the lawyer who handled the adoption, but he was dead and the law office he worked for couldn't find any of the paperwork." She shook her head. "Knowing my aunt, she had the whole thing burned in case I changed my mind. But she couldn't keep me from putting my name and all the information I had on the national registry."

"What registry?"

"Online. There's a sort of clearinghouse for adopted children and birth parents."

"Did you put my name on the list?"

"No," she exclaimed, her tone scandalized. "Of course not."

"Why? Because you couldn't prove I was the father?"

"Because you didn't know about him. I imagined all sorts of terrible scenarios if he showed up at your doorstep, first."

He could picture the chaos that might have caused—a bit like learning the kid you called your son wasn't your son.

"You never got a hit." It wasn't a question. Her sad, wistful look was answer enough.

"I was going to give him two more years. I figured by his first year in college he ought to have figured out whether or not he wanted to know about his birth parents."

"And if he never called? What then?"

She didn't answer. "More coffee?"

"No, thanks. Before I make up my mind about what to do, I'd like to see the paperwork on the birth."

She nodded and got up. "Do you wanna wait here or come? It's probably a little cold."

He stood, too. Did she really think he trusted her to give him proof without him watching her every move?

She rolled her eyes the way his daughters would have. "Oh, Daddy, get over yourself," they liked to say. Char didn't speak. She walked to the hall closet and grabbed a coat—the same bright purple one from yesterday. "There's a man's parka in there that might fit. Someone left it in the store and never came back for it."

He knew immediately which one she meant but getting it out was no easy task. The rack was stuffed tight. He slipped it on over his sweatshirt and hurried after her. The snow had stopped but the first bite of cold air reminded him of waking up in the Badlands.

Badlands. Vision quest. Missing piece. Was there any chance his destiny—if he believed in such things—was tied to this woman's?

She ignored the shovel resting against the side

of the building and marched through the snow on the sidewalk between the house and the rear entrance of the log building. The teepee and auxiliary corridor that connected the two edifices sat at an angle favoring the parking lot.

"Be my guest," she said, after unlocking the metal door. "The light switch is on the right, but brace yourself," she warned, "I have my assistant turn down the heat when she closes for me."

She wasn't kidding. He could see his breath in the frosty air.

She followed him in, gesturing for him to stay on the customer side of the counter while she opened the safe. She dropped out of sight for a moment.

Eli shifted from side to side, his toes curling to keep warm. He happened to look down and noticed something on the floor. A feather. He leaned over and picked it up.

Small. Not much bigger than his thumb. Black for about half an inch. Smooth. Shiny. The white part closest to the quill was soft and downy.

He looked around, wondering where it came from. One of the ceremonial headdresses, he guessed, which even from a distance appeared meticulously—and authentically—detailed. Or perhaps someone had purchased one of the dream catchers he'd noticed the day before. He had to admit there wasn't a cheesy, foreign souvenir in sight. He owed her an apology.

"Here it is," she said, popping to her feet.

She set a standard-size manila file folder on the counter between them.

He tucked the little feather into his pocket. He couldn't bear the thought of people walking on it. How ridiculous was that? Was he still tripping out or what?

"The kid's almost reached the age of consent. How come your aunt won't tell you anything?"

"I…um…haven't brought up the subject in over a year. The last time I asked, she went off about some newspaper article she'd read. Supposedly a tribe back east gained custody of a child who had been adopted by a loving, non-Native American family. The battle went to court and the tribe won. According to my aunt, the child was going to become a ward of the tribe and would be raised in foster care."

"Keeping the tribal rolls up is a problem in some areas, especially in places near or below poverty level. But that's pretty much a moot point for a seventeen-year-old, isn't it?"

"Did I say I agreed with her? Unfortunately Pam got so worked up she had to be sedated. Her partner, Carlinda, asked me not to speak of the adoption again in front of Pam."

He waited, sensing there was more. "Another dead end."

She shrugged. "I didn't say this was going to

be easy." She pointed to the file in his hand. "Take a look for yourself. Maybe you'll see something I've missed. I'm going to check my online auctions." He spotted her computer a few feet away. "You can take that back to the house, if you want to warm up."

He wasn't ready to leave her, but not because he didn't trust her. "I saw a chair in the teepee yesterday. Can I go in there?"

She blinked in surprise. "Feel free…if you're prepared to freeze your very fine…um…" Her gaze dropped for the briefest moment to his derriere. He couldn't call her look ogling, but that small slip pretty much confirmed that her reaction to his kiss yesterday hadn't been a fluke. The lingering look here…offhand touch there… that he'd tried to write off as his imagination was real. She was attracted to him on a level that had nothing to do with finding their kid. Or was she clinging to some girlish fantasy for a guy who didn't exist?

His mortally wounded ego urged him to throw caution to the wind and find out. Fortunately the responsible cop part of his brain was back in control. He could—and would—ignore the undercurrent of pheromones zipping between them.

Without a word, he walked to the Navajo rugs and slipped through the opening. The temperature in the hallway dropped a good twenty degrees. Better than a cold shower any day, he told himself.

"There's a freestanding heater beside the chair," she called, poking her head in after him. "Hit the on button and turn the fan to high. You won't freeze to death. I promise."

He flashed the universal sign for okay then quickly shoved his hand in the pocket of his borrowed coat. A minute later, he plopped into the large, upholstered chair and pulled a buffalo hide blanket across his lap. The muted roar of the heater quickly began to dispel the cold.

After blowing on his fingers, he opened the file and began to read. He started with the journal she'd included. A different one than he'd seen yesterday. The handwriting was the same, but the tone was different. More grown-up. The official documents backed up her story, but the only proof that he was the father of her child was missing. As she'd admitted, his name didn't appear on the birth certificate. There wasn't a court in the land that would have held him responsible without more substantial evidence.

He got up, turned off the heater and returned to the shop. He glanced at the wall clock, surprised to see an hour had passed. The shop was warmer now. Her coat hung from a peg near the door. She was seated at her computer, her back to him. When he tossed the folder on the counter, she jumped in a way that told him she hadn't heard him approach.

She quickly collected herself and stood up. "So?"

"Without a kid and a DNA test you got nothing," he said, wishing he actually believed that.

She glanced at her computer and back. "He said you'd say that."

"He?"

"Your uncle," she said. "He e-mailed me. Or maybe his girlfriend did. It came from her e-mail address."

Eli shook his head. "What the hell are you talking about?"

She grabbed his sleeve and pulled him into the small space beside her. "Look," she said, pointing at the screen. "The header says Eli Robideaux's uncle. I already opened the document he attached. If you click on the icon at the bottom of the page, you can see that, too."

That oh-crap feeling in the pit of his stomach was brewing again. Was this part of some sort of conspiracy? When had his uncle picked up computer skills? Did Joseph's broad hints about a big white teepee and missing pieces of his soul mean he had inside information? How? Why deliver it now? Was Char in on it?

He read the message standing up. It wasn't long.

Tell my nephew when you see him to trust the truth. He knows it. So do you. The healer has the name you seek.

"Who's the healer?"

"My aunt, I assume."

With his heart in his throat, he clicked on the little icon that indicated an attachment. A certificate of live birth. Char reached past him to hit the zoom button.

The image matched the one he'd been holding a few minutes earlier, except you could tell this one had been crumpled at one time.

She scrolled down and hit the zoom again.

He inhaled sharply. On the line left for father was his name.

"I told you I don't lie."

He couldn't look at her. He didn't know what this meant in the grand scheme of things, or what he was supposed to do about the news. He turned and walked back into the teepee, stopping when he got to the center. Pulse racing, his mind a whirl, he looked upward. He could see a piece of sky in the opening where the support poles crossed. A few snowflakes filtered in.

I have a son.

Somewhere in the world was a boy—a young

man—only a few months younger than E.J. Eli's flesh and blood. History and reality.

A boy who needs his father, chickadee.

Eli blinked, startled by the voice that sounded so clear he scanned the teepee for speakers. But the voice wasn't Char's. Female, yes, but it had a funny, Southern accent.

A gust of wind made a shiver course down his spine. He looked up again. His breath caught in his throat as he watched a small bird alight on the lip of the canvas material. A wren? It had to be a wren. There were thousands of them. Winter and summer, they weren't migra—

Before he could complete the thought the little bird swept downward, as if dropping by for a visit. It didn't seem panicked about being inside. In fact, it circled a couple of times then landed on a freestanding globe a foot or so away.

His breathing stopped. He could see it quite clearly now. The same black-capped bird from his narcotic-induced sweat lodge vision. "You're not real," he murmured, shaking his head.

An irreverent cackle echoed in his brain. *Real enough, chickadee.*

The bird cocked its head to look at him.

"Oh, shit. I'm losing my mind."

He didn't believe in signs. He got the fact that his uncle, who once worked in the janitorial department of the Pierre hospital, might have stumbled across a discarded birth certificate and sat on it all these years, thinking he was doing Eli a favor. He could even picture Joseph setting up this vision quest as a way to shake Eli out of his funk. But birds and voices…no way.

"No way what?" Char asked.

He hadn't realized he spoke out loud. Nor had he noticed her standing there. She was a yard or so away, but obviously too focused on him to notice the bird. Hands on hips, she seemed visibly upset.

"What's it going to take to get you to believe me? If this isn't proof enough—" she held up a printed copy of the birth certificate "—then screw you. I'm going to find our son—with or without your help."

She turned on one heel and stomped out of the teepee at the same instant the bird shot skyward. It cleared the small opening without any trouble and was gone from view as if it had never existed.

Eli's fingers tingled from the residual adrenaline left in his system. His mouth was bone-dry. His knees felt as if they might give out. He reached for the globe to get his balance.

After a few moments he felt more like himself. This was crazy. Joseph wasn't in touch with the Great Spirit who sent a chickadee to give him some kind of message.

He needed to leave. Go back to his life. Make

peace with Bobbi and his daughters. Mend fences with E.J. Get his job back. Those were the pieces of his life that needed his attention.

He'd give Char his blessing. His apology, if that would help. He couldn't accompany her on a wild-goose chase tracking down a seventeen-year-old boy who most probably was living an average life in relative peace and harmony.

He took in a deep breath and slowly let it out. As he did, he looked down. The globe was tilted on its axis, making the predominant visual point the Pacific coast of North America. But something didn't look right. He leaned closer, squinting.

He jerked back suddenly when he realized what he was looking at. San Francisco Bay wasn't a bay anymore. It had been filled in with bird poop.

A deep, unexpected laughter worked its way up his throat. Tears filled his eyes as he doubled over, gasping for breath.

Char raced back. "What?"

Holding his side, he pointed. "Shit," he managed to get out before doubling over again.

She stared at him as though he'd lost his mind. Which he probably had. But even if you weren't the kind of guy who believed in signs, some were irrefutable.

CHAPTER SEVEN

"COULD YOU LEND ME SOME money?"

Char was standing at the front window of her shop, peering at the empty parking lot. He could read the open sign beside her shoulder, which, obviously, meant she'd decided to remain closed, even though the snow was letting up.

"So you can leave?" she asked, turning to face him. She didn't seem as upset as she had earlier. His laughing fit might have made her question the wisdom of including him in her search for their child.

Eli hated being on the receiving end of generosity, but if he was going to do this, he needed cash—something his uncle had managed to alleviate him of. "I'll pay you back. Or work for it. I could shovel the parking lot." He started toward her. "But I'm gonna need a bit more than that to get to the West Coast."

Her jaw dropped and she eyed him warily. He didn't blame her. She'd been kind and helpful to the extreme and he'd been a surly, disagreeable jerk.

"What changed your mind?"

"A small bird."

"Did it tell you to go to California and talk my aunt into giving you the name of the family that adopted our son?"

He made a wobbly motion with his hand. "Sorta."

She didn't seem shocked or ready to call someone to take him away. "Then you believe me."

He didn't want to but how could he not? "Yes."

She blew out a sigh that sounded relieved, but a moment later she frowned. "Unfortunately we may be too late. Pam's memory has gotten really bad. I don't think she knew me the last time I visited."

"She's not that old, is she?"

"Seventy. She started having seizures about eight years ago. Out of the blue. No one seems to know why. Her doctors were able to control them with drugs but one of the side effects was memory loss. Pam had to quit working, couldn't drive a car. That led to depression. There was an accidental overdose…" Her voice trailed off. "The Alzheimer's diagnosis is recent."

Eli had had some experience on the job with elderly residents wandering away from the family home. The Lakota revered their elders and rarely farmed them out to clinical care facilities, but given how busy most families were these days, that sometimes meant less observation rather than more.

"The last time I was there, she kept calling me Glory. My mom's nickname," she added.

"I've interrogated a lot of people who didn't want to tell me stuff. Maybe your aunt will open up for me."

She didn't say anything right away, but she looked thoughtful. After a minute or so, she said, "The first step is finding a flight. Whenever I want to do something impulsive, I let luck guide me. If you go online and there's an affordable flight with two seats, then you know this trip was meant to be."

"You're going, too?"

She took a step closer. Her fresh, amazing scent filled his nostrils. "He's my kid, too," she said, stomping her foot. "If you're going, I'm going. Especially, if we're using my credit card."

She had a point. One he couldn't very well argue with, but that didn't stop him from wondering what happened to the shy, retiring girl who was content to hang out in the background.

She grew up in a hurry.

The voice again. But this time it sounded more like his conscience. He shrugged and put a comfortable distance between them—one that wouldn't make it easy for him to reel her into his arms and finish that kiss they'd started. "Your dime, your call."

CHAR WASN'T SURPRISED by how smoothly things came together. As she'd told Eli, if you were on the right path, the universe nudged aside obstacles.

Take the matter of hiring someone to operate the store in her absence. Yes, Char could count on Pia for part of the time, but the younger woman really wasn't cut out for taking charge. And, yes, Char could close the store, but she didn't want to lose money if she could avoid it.

"You need someone to be you for a few days?" Kat had replied when Char phoned her. Kat had been first on Char's list because historically Kat had always been scrambling for extra money and Char had hoped she might be able to handle the coming weekend…if Char was gone that long. "I have the perfect person," Kat exclaimed. "Jack's sister, Rachel. She's going through a post-divorce rough spell, plus she lost her job to the depressed housing market. Jack finally talked her into coming to Sentinel Pass to check things out. What better way to meet people than to manage Native Arts?"

Char made Rachel her next call and, sure enough, the woman sounded perfect. She seemed to share Jack's business sense and work ethic. That was good enough for Char. And, even better, Rachel was available immediately.

"Hire a replacement? Done," Char said aloud as she crossed the biggest hurdle off her list.

The next item should have been less challenging, but Char's hand was shaking as she punched in her aunt's phone number. She didn't know whether to be relieved or annoyed to reach an answering machine, but she left a message. Short and to the point.

"Hi, dear ladies. This is Char. I'm going to be in town hopefully tomorrow. Let me know the best time to come by and see you. Here's my cell phone number, in case you don't have it." She rattled off the pertinent information and hung up.

"How'd you know we'd be able to get out tonight?" a masculine voice asked.

She ignored the flutter in her chest cavity—now wasn't the time to get sick or give in to girlish nonsense. "I've taken the red-eye several times. Not the most pleasant way to travel but there are usually seats up for grab. Did you try Priceline?"

As they discussed their agenda and the cost of their tickets, Char tried to pay attention but her mind wouldn't cooperate. She didn't doubt for a minute that Eli would pay her back. But if for some reason he didn't, she could afford to absorb the cost of the room at the boutique hotel where she'd stayed before. And the cost of their B.A.R.T. tickets, which would take them from the Oakland airport into the city. But right below the surface of her businesslike demeanor was a girl shrieking in wonder and dismay. Wonder that she was traveling with Eli—her Eli—to find the baby boy—her baby boy—she'd given up for adoption. Dismay that she was still Char Jones—the girl who had no self-control when it came to Eli Robideaux.

"What are we going to do from the time we get in until we can check in at the hotel?" Eli asked. He was standing behind her looking over her shoulder at every click of the mouse. His scent, his presence, his freakin' swoo was more than she could take.

She held up her hand. "Stop. Back up." He didn't move. "I mean that literally. Take a step backward. You're crowding my space. I've been on my own for a long, long time. I travel alone. I run my business alone. I can make these plans without you breathing down my neck."

He held up his hands mockingly and put a single giant step between them. "Excuse me. I'm the kind of person who likes to know in advance what is happening."

"A micromanager. I get that. But yesterday, we were virtual strangers and now you know my credit card number. It's possible we're getting ahead of ourselves here."

He inhaled deeply. "Yes. And no."

She cocked her head, waiting for an explanation.

"Going to San Francisco might be a wild-goose chase. Your aunt may have forgotten anything that could help us. But what if she kept records that you don't know about? You got the habit of writing a journal from someone, right?"

Char hadn't thought of that. "How come you're not working? And if we're going to be traveling together I think I deserve to know exactly what's going on with you and Bobbi."

He acknowledged her demand with a tilt of his head. "I took a leave of absence from my job. Bobbi filed for a divorce in July. She and the girls are living with her folks in Reliance. E.J.—my, um…son, Eli, Jr.—is living in Pierre with some friends."

She knew there was more to the story. Eighteen-year marriages didn't simply fall apart. But it wasn't her business. Not really. They might share a child, but that was all they had in common.

"Have you considered what will happen if we actually find him? I mean, where your other kids are concerned?"

His blue eyes turned as flinty as ice chips. "A

minute ago you were certain we'd never get a bit of information out of your aunt. Let me worry about integrating the missing piece into the family fold. Such as it is."

She was sorry to hear such bitterness in his voice, but she guessed that part of his attitude stemmed from the wound to his ego, so she returned to her task of finding the best price for a rental car—in case they needed one.

They maintained their uneasy truce until the phone rang. Char picked it up and answered, "Native Arts."

"Char? It's me, Libby. I just talked to Kat. She said you're going to California."

She turned to Eli. "Friends," she said, knowing Libby could hear, too. "Can't live without them, can't get away with anything around them."

"I'm not prying," Libby scolded her. "I wanted to see if you'd be there long enough to come see Cooper and me. We're headed back on Tuesday. We're going to host our first Thanksgiving at the beach house. You're invited, of course."

Char picked up the portable unit and left the much-too-small confines of the office area. At the large picture window, she leaned her shoulder against the frame and looked outside. The wind had come up; long fingers of snow formed triangular drifts across the parking lot.

"I doubt if we'll be gone that long, but thanks for asking."

"We?"

Truth and consequence time. "Eli—the old friend I told you about—and I are flying out tonight provided the plane can get off the ground." To forestall the obvious question, she quickly added, "We have business together. Old business. I'm not ready to talk about it, okay?"

"Of course." Char could hear Libby's unspoken worry, but Libby, being Libby, gave Char the space she needed. "Just keep your cell handy and call if we can help in any way. And, according to the weather station, this front should blow itself out in the next hour or so. A melt is predicted by tomorrow."

Char smiled. Typical Black Hills weather. "Good. Then I don't have to hire Mac to clear the parking lot."

They talked a few minutes longer. Until a curious sound caught Char's attention. Scraping. She walked to the window on the opposite side of the building. A man in black was shoveling the sidewalk leading to the garage.

Either he was an optimist or he sensed that the storm was almost over and normal traffic might resume. *Maybe he's working off the price of his airplane ticket, chickadee.*

"Char? Are you still there?"

Physically, maybe. Mentally…not so much. "Yeah. Sorry."

"I just wanted to repeat my invitation for Thanksgiving. You know it's my favorite holiday, and this will be the first time I've celebrated outside of Sentinel Pass. I feel homesick already and I haven't even left. I'd really love it if you could come. Jenna and Shane will be there, and Mac and Morgan, too. Think about it, okay?"

It took some effort, but Char made herself stop staring at Eli. She marched to the Brulé wall calendar and counted the days. "Nope. No way can I afford to be gone that long. Sorry, Lib. But if you tell me Coop's going to deep fry a turkey, I might change my mind. Sounds like a YouTube moment for sure."

Libby laughed. "It does, doesn't it? Well, I won't count on you, but I won't count you out until I have to. Your business with your old flame might take longer than you think."

"Who said he was a flame?"

"Char, I may be pregnant, but I'm not blind. I could tell the moment you walked in the door that he was someone special."

Special. Talk about an understatement. The physical attraction that got her into this situation in the first place hadn't diminished over the years. If anything, it was stronger. But she wasn't some giddy girl with a serious crush. She'd had plenty of time to figure out what she wanted in a man, a mate. Right up there at the top of the list was emotional stability. A requirement that would certainly preclude a guy who was in the traumatic process of ending his marriage.

As a devotee of *People* magazine, over the years she'd seen more than a few rebound flings wind up discarded and broken when the rejected guy they'd fallen for was drawn like flotsam in a tractor beam back to the woman who had rejected him in the first place. Char didn't know why they went back, but they always did.

She needed to remember that because in a few hours she'd be on a plane to San Francisco with the hunkiest rejected guy on the planet—after a quick stop at Target to pick up a couple of changes of clothes for her temporarily homeless friend.

"Lib, I do have one favor to ask. Remember that checklist I made for you when you filled in for me the last time I went to visit my aunt?"

"Yeah. It really helped."

"If I print out a copy, could you walk Jack's sister through the basics? I could ask Pia, but her feelings might be hurt that I didn't ask her to cover for me."

"Of course. No problem. Don't worry about a thing. Rachel will take good care of your baby."

Char hung up a few minutes later, but Libby's

words stayed in her mind. The sad fact was her business had become her whole world.

And now that world was changing. Scary as that felt Char told herself she'd be okay as long as she remembered who she was and where she came from. Her teepee would still be here when she returned.

CHAPTER EIGHT

CHAR LOVED SAN FRANCISCO. For a gal straight from Hicksville, she'd never felt intimidated or out of place in this city. Probably because quirky was this town's middle name.

"We're getting off at the next stop," she told Eli, who was sitting beside her in the B.A.R.T train that had just transported them under the waters of the bay. They'd arrived at the Oakland Airport just as the first fingers of dawn pried back the curtain of night.

Early morning commuters, laden with tall, insulated mugs of coffee, earbuds and newspapers made up most of the other passengers. Char was tired but she couldn't suppress a niggling sense of excitement. Not only was she about to enter one of her favorite places on the planet, but she had a companion. That almost never happened.

Unless you counted the voice in her head, Char was always alone. But not today.

The train came to a smooth stop, the doors opening on a hiss. Eli shouldered the canvas backpack she'd loaned him and offered her a hand. She took it. Why not?

You know why not, chickadee. You like his touch too much.

"Do you have your ticket ready? You have to put it in the machine to get out."

"Really? But we bought round-trip passes."

She towed her small, black wheelie bag behind her. "It'll come back out. Watch."

She led the way through the cattle gates, as she called them, and pointed toward the nearest staircase. "Our hotel is that way," she said once they reached Market Street. "The clerk I spoke with said we could probably check in around noon."

He slid back the cuff of his heavy jacket. His watch was an old one of Char's. One she'd bought online and felt was too mannish once she got it. "Too early to burst in on your aunt, I suppose. Breakfast?"

She'd packed them food for the trip, but the two remaining power bars didn't sound very appealing at the moment. "Coffee, for sure," she said. "I know a place around the corner from Pam's. It's a bit of a hike, but after being scrunched up in a plane overnight, a walk sounds good to me. Are you up for it?"

He gave her one of his inscrutable looks and nodded.

"Indian men," she muttered, starting for the corner. She didn't jaywalk. Her first trip here, she'd nearly been creamed by a messenger on a bike. Since then she'd become a model pedestrian.

The sheer volume of people hurrying along the sidewalk kept conversation at a minimum. They didn't actually have a chance to speak until they were seated at a tiny table in the corner café. The glass windows were steamed over around the edges. At home, Char could have called it the lace effect.

"What did you mean when you called me an Indian man?"

She looked up from the laminated menu. Nothing was cheap in this town, but she no longer griped about the cost out loud. Her aunt once told her such complaining only proved she was a tourist.

"Did I offend you? Sorry. I should have said Native American men. Or do you prefer Indigenous Peoples?"

He scowled. "I couldn't give a crap about what's P.C. I meant what did you mean by the comment?"

"Oh. Well, I've had hundreds of dealings with men of your tribe over the years and I've learned that half the time they only tell you what they think you want to hear. The other half, they lie."

He stared in shocked silence for a few seconds

then burst out laughing. A first. She liked the sound. Deep and masculine. "Actually that's pretty astute. But I'm only half-Native."

"I know."

"You do?"

She folded the menu and set it aside. "I had a huge crush on you, remember? And I was a student helper in the principal's office."

"You accessed my records?"

A harried blonde in a retro pink and black uniform paused long enough to give Eli the once-over and take their order before disappearing into the crowded restaurant. Char didn't like the momentary clutch of jealousy she experienced. "Never date a guy who's cuter than you are," her mother once warned. "All the even cuter girls will try to steal him away."

That was about the sum total of her mother's maternal advice. And it certainly had proven true more than once when Mom made the wrong choice from the dating pool.

"I didn't have access to anyone's records. I just listened and maybe asked a question or two. You know how people like to gossip. My family got talked about enough."

"What did you learn?"

She poured cream from a stainless steel pitcher into her cup and stirred, watching it turn the mixture the color of her grandmother's pine rocking chair. "Well, they said your maternal grandfather was your dad's commanding officer in the army. Your dad and mom eloped and he nearly got court-martialed for going AWOL."

"True. He took a less-than-honorable discharge and moved back home."

"They said your mom hated the reservation. She lasted a couple of winters then moved to Texas or Oklahoma."

"Oklahoma. My grandmother lived there. She'd divorced my grandfather shortly before I was born. Mom said Granny got fed up with the way Gramps handled things with my mom and dad."

"That's where you lived during the school year, but you spent your summers in Lower Brule."

"Mom remarried when I was six. My stepdad, Carl, had two kids. They were a few years older than me and they lived with their mother most of the time. We were never close. Then the twins were born. Sara and Mike. After Mom died, Carl had a pretty rough time keeping it all together. Dad invited me to come live with him. He convinced me I'd have a shot at some college scholarships if I traded on my ethnicity and went to Pierre High."

"Do you see your half siblings much?"

"Mike's in Iraq at the moment. Works for a private contractor. But Sara's a sweetheart. She's happily married with two kids. We e-mail each other quite a bit."

He frowned. "She's probably starting to get worried. I haven't e-mailed her since last week. Normally she would have called Bobbi to find out what was up, but Sara's loyal to the max. She was furious when she heard the news."

"It's probably none of my business, but can I ask what went wrong between you two?"

He brushed back an errant strand of hair from his furrowed brow. "The usual."

"Another man?" she croaked, louder than she'd planned. Ducking her head slightly, she whispered, "I don't believe it. Who could she…?"

A memory she'd completely forgotten popped into her mind. Bobbi and a dark-haired guy who wasn't Eli making out under the bleachers after a home game. "Robert?" she mouthed.

"Yeah. Apparently they had more in common than they knew."

Like us? She didn't ask the question because their server returned at that moment with their food. Scrambled eggs and fruit for Char; eggs Benedict for Eli.

As the woman refilled their mugs, she studied Char. "I like your hair. Very autumnal."

Self-consciously, Char touched her uncombed mop. She was aware of Eli looking at her. He'd called her odd. Did he still feel that way?

They ate in silence until Char couldn't contain her curiosity any longer. "So what happened? They were apart for all these years then suddenly got back together? Can you talk about it?"

He took a bite and chewed. "I could, but I'm not going to. Know why?"

She moved her chin from side to side.

"Because I'd either tell you what I think you want to hear…or I'd lie."

She hid her smile with her mug. *He got you that time, chickadee. Hooeee, I do believe I like this boy.*

Me, too, Char agreed. *Me, too.*

ELI HAD NEVER BEEN to San Francisco, but he didn't expect to like it. The freaking air temperature felt colder than the snowy clime he'd just left even though a big sign on a billboard claimed it was fifty degrees.

And the damp moisture that wasn't rain—according to Char—collected on his eyelashes and cheeks, making his nose drip.

"You don't like the fog, do you?"

He also hated being transparent. He didn't answer.

"Don't get surly. I'm not in charge of the weather. Besides, the fog will burn off in a little while and then it'll be warm and sunny."

He didn't believe her. And how did someone

like her get to be so city smart? He didn't ask because the more he learned about her life, the more he liked her. Like led to friendly, friendly led to knoodling, knoodling was the first step on a slippery slope that would surely lead to a bad, bad ending. Another bad ending. One was enough.

"Here we are," she said, her cheerful voice breaking through his attitude, as bleak and cheerless as the sky.

She stopped before a waist-high wrought-iron gate. The unusual fence appeared to be made out of old metal headboards—some painted, some rusting.

"Are those…?"

"Uh-huh. Some of these headboards supposedly were pulled from the debris of the 1910 earthquake. I adore the Painted Ladies."

He looked up at the narrow, three-story corner home. The house appeared to be touching a similar home on its left. The right side followed the street, and he could see a tiny garage set under the home. "Is your aunt's partner rich?"

Char's shoulders lifted and fell. "Carlinda's family owns another place on Nob Hill. But don't worry. Carly's not a snob. She's a surgeon, a teacher and a political activist for gay rights. She's amazing."

Eli followed her through the gate. While she

climbed the steep steps to ring the bell, he studied the building's unusual paint job. He didn't know how purple, green, orange and a couple of other odd shades he couldn't name managed to look complementary, but the combination worked on this impressive-looking structure.

"Char," exclaimed the tall woman who opened the door. "Welcome, dear heart." A gust of air made the woman's long, wavy silver hair fly about in every direction. She brushed it away impatiently. "Come in. Come in. Pam is so excited about your visit. She actually seemed to understand who was coming. It might be the new meds. It might be you."

Once inside the huge, two- or three-story entry, the two exchanged a long, obviously heartfelt hug. "Carly, this is Eli. He and I were in school together."

"Ah…" the woman said, her lively green eyes checking him out from head to toe. "The plot thickens." She shook his hand, firmly but warmly. "I knew there had to be a man involved. Char is never this impulsive."

Eli looked around, hoping he didn't make a fool of himself by gaping, open-jawed. The place was a real-life mansion, complete with white marble floors, a dramatic winding staircase and a gigantic crystal candelabra-type light fixture that looked like it had been there forever.

"I'm so sorry we don't have a bed to offer you," Carly was saying when Eli tuned back into the conversation she was having with Char. "Our exchange student's family is visiting from Honduras. You just missed them. They're doing Alcatraz this morning."

She looked at Eli as if intending to say more. He braced himself for a comment about the notorious prison's occupation by members of the American Indian Movement, but she didn't. Eli was grateful. For one thing, that part of his father's people's history was long before Eli's time. For another, he hated it when strangers made assumptions about him based on his ethnicity.

"No problem," Char said, shrugging off her coat. She'd left the bright purple one at home, opting for a more practical black slicker-type with a hood. Eli sorta missed her bold colors. Demure didn't go with her hair. "As I told you on the phone, this isn't a pleasure trip. It might even be a wild-goose chase, depending on what Pam tells us."

Carly, who was dressed in black wool pants and a white sweater that looked casual but probably would have taken the better part of Eli's last paycheck to buy, reached out and touched Char's arm. "I wish I could be more encouraging, honey. The new drug she's taking seems to target the short-term memory. She's able to maintain a more even keel on a day-to-day basis, but I haven't seen any great improvement in her long-term memory."

Char looked at him. "That's what I told Eli, but he was hoping Pam might have saved some old files or paperwork from the early 1990s."

Their hostess looked thoughtful. "Well…there might be some of that sort of thing down in the basement. You know what a pack rat your auntie always was. Just like you, if I remember correctly."

Eli pictured Char's cluttered hall closet and nodded. She gave him a stern look that made him bite back a smile. Her secret faults were minor compared to some people's. His ex-wife's, for example.

Char opened her purse that doubled as a backpack and dug around a moment. "I brought some goodies. Buffalo jerky and chokecherry jelly." She'd transferred the latter out of her checked luggage at the café. "You can dazzle your South American guests when they come back."

Carly seemed genuinely delighted. She motioned for them to follow her down a short hall to a bright, high-ceiling kitchen. The yellow walls and black and white tile looked like something Eli might have found in the pages of the home-decorating magazines Bobbi adored.

"Coffee?"

Both Char and Eli declined.

"Well, sweets, I hate to run off, but I have a meeting at the hospital this morning. Your aunt's upstairs. We have a practical nurse who looks after her during the day. She takes Pam for walks and drives her to therapy. Her name is—"

Suddenly she stopped. Her polished facade dissolved and she reached out for the counter to keep from crumpling. Char rushed to her side.

"Carlinda? Are you okay?"

The older woman took several deep breaths and gave a weak smile. "Yes. I'm fine. Healthy, if that's what you mean. But emotionally I'm very close to the edge. As a doctor, I know that caregivers often suffer from depression and are prone to breakdowns. I honestly didn't think it would apply to me because I have a financial cushion and a wonderful support system of friends and family. But…" She looked up tearfully. "None of that helps when you're watching the person you love disappear behind a cloud that you're powerless to obliterate."

Char rubbed her back supportively. "I'm sorry."

"Me, too," Carly said. "I lied earlier. I'm not going to a meeting at the hospital. I've decided to move your aunt to a full care facility. Her primary physician has been advocating this for several months, but I couldn't bring myself to consider it."

Eli looked at Char to see her reaction to the news. "To be honest, Carly, I expected this months ago. You've got nothing to feel guilty about. I only wish there was more I could do. If you need me to stay…"

Carlinda shook her head. "You're a doll. Thanks for offering, but everyone says it's best for the patient if we make this a clean break. Once Pam enters the home, I'm taking a cruise through the Greek isles."

The two embraced then, heads touching. "You've fought this disease with every weapon in your arsenal, Carly. Now it's time for Pam to follow her path, and you to stay on yours. No one will judge you for that."

The self-imposed locks Eli had clamped over his heart sprang open like a child's jack-in-the-box toy. He'd never met anyone as kind and generous of spirit as Char. He liked her. A lot.

But it was also clear a few minutes later when they entered a spectacular suite of rooms on the second floor with a knock-your-socks-off view of the Bay Bridge that Char's patience and goodwill didn't extend quite as magnanimously to her aunt.

"Hi, Aunt Pam," Char said cordially. "It's me. Charlene."

There was a nasally twang to her pronunciation

that he'd never heard before. "How are you? Same great view. Boy, I bet this never grows old, huh?"

She walked straight to the whiskey-color leather chair where a small, stocky woman with short gray hair was sitting. Dressed in a navy-blue jogging suit and Uggs, her aunt appeared as normal as any of them. Until she turned her head to look in their direction. Then Eli saw that something was missing. Any spark of recognition for one thing.

A woman in her mid-forties wearing baggy white pants and a brightly colored smock acknowledged them from the doorway of an adjoining room but pointed to the cell phone she had to her ear. Eli had the feeling the call was from one story below them. The nurse gave a little wave and closed the door between the two rooms.

Eli appreciated the privacy. Bad enough he had to interview a woman who was obviously in a place far, far away from reality without airing his and Char's dirty laundry for a crowd.

"Aunt Pam, I brought someone along to see you. This is Eli Robideaux. He went to school with me. Back in South Dakota," she added, motioning him closer.

He took off his jacket and joined Char on the leather sofa adjacent to her aunt's chair. The grouping was situated to take advantage of the view.

"Hello, Miss Jones. Nice to see you again."

"Miss Jones?" her aunt repeated. She looked at Char in obvious confusion.

"That's your last name, Auntie. Pam Jones."

"Pamela Edwina. After my father."

Char looked at him in surprise. "That's right. Granddad's name was Edward. I'd forgotten. Do you remember my mother's name? Your baby sister."

"Charlene?"

"Nope. That's me. My mother's name was Gloria. You called her Glory."

The tiny glimmer in the woman's eyes went out.

Char made a couple more attempts to connect with her aunt, but it was obvious to Eli that her patience had been tapped out.

He cleared his throat. "I think I could use another cup of coffee, if the offer is still open."

"You're trying to get rid of me, aren't you?"

"I'm giving you an out before you turn into the bad cop."

Her smile seemed genuine again. "I keep remembering the way she was. 'A force to be reckoned with,' my mom used to call her. Once Pam decided on a course of action, there was no stopping her."

He heard a hint of anguish in her tone.

"You make her sound like a bully."

Char stared at the woman who appeared to have no interest in them whatsoever. Pam's gaze never left the horizon, which was finally showing hints of sunlight as the fog burned off.

"Honestly? I hated her for a really long time. When Mom married her last husband and moved to Arizona, I moved in with my girlfriend's family rather than live alone in the same house with Pam." She looked at her aunt for several heartbeats, then she sat up straighter and added, "In hindsight, that was probably mean, but it all worked out for the best. Pam met Carlinda at a medical conference and a few months later sold Grandma's house and moved. She shared the money equally with Mom, Aunt Marilyn and me. She didn't have to, but she did."

"Out of guilt?"

She shrugged. "I doubt it." To her aunt, she asked, "You never felt guilty about anything you did, did you?"

"Nope," Pam answered, almost as if she knew what she was saying.

Char lingered a few minutes longer then jumped to her feet and hurried away. Eli scooted over to where she'd been sitting so he could face her aunt directly. Char's warmth lingered on the leather and he savored the sensation for the tiniest of moments before reaching out to take the woman's hands.

In a strange way, the disease that had ravaged Pam's mind made her appear younger than Carlinda, who according to Char was the same age as her aunt. Everyday stress and worry was gone from Pam's face. She seemed placid, lost in some other world beyond the veil.

"Pam," he said. "I don't expect you to remember me, but you do remember being a nurse-practitioner, don't you? People counted on you to fix them up. I need your help now, Pam. Char had a baby boy. You were there for her. Can you think back to that time, Pam? When you lived in Pierre."

"Pierre is the capital of South Dakota."

A tiny zigzag of hope skittered through his extremities. He squeezed her hands gently. "That's right. You lived there. You took care of people. You helped Charlene give birth to your great-nephew."

She looked straight into his eyes. "Black hair and blue eyes. Strangest thing I ever saw."

Eli was reluctant to breathe for fear he'd lose their connection. "Who'd you give him to, Pam?"

Her gaze started to drift away. He squeezed her hands a tiny bit tighter.

"He flew away."

"The baby?"

"The captain. He took the baby and flew away."

The captain? A pilot? Maybe in the Air Force?

"What was the captain's name? Do you remember?" Going on gut instinct he started rattling off men's names. "John. Mark. Paul. Robert. Tony."

Her eyes widened a bit. "Italian." She leaned forward and whispered, "Don't tell Charlene. She made me promise he was Indian. Like you."

The blood in Eli's ears rushed noisily as adrenaline shot into his system. He might not have a name, but he had a start. And that was a helluva lot more than he'd had ten minutes ago.

She yanked her hands away and tried to get up. He could tell her balance wasn't quite right. "Um…hello? Nurse? Help?"

The door to the next room opened and the attending nurse hurried over. "There you are, Pam. Are you ready for your walk? I hope so. The sun is out and I need some fresh air. But you still need a coat, my dear. No arguments."

Eli moved out of the way and smiled his gratitude as the woman helped her charge toward the hall. They paused to let Char enter. Char set down the cup she was carrying and gave her aunt a light hug. A moment later, she joined him.

"See?" she said, pointing to the view. "I told you the sun would come out."

He took a drink of coffee. High-end. Better than the cup that cost them four bucks. "Does the hotel you booked have WiFi?"

She nodded. "Why?"

"We have a name. Sorta. Maybe." He didn't want to get her hopes up. "I wouldn't take it to court, but my gut says it's a lead worth following."

She looked at him, a bemused smile on her lips. "Well, then, let's go. And you know the best part?"

He shook his head.

"It's downhill all the way...to the hotel," she added with a hint of mischief.

CHAPTER NINE

THEY HAD A NAME.

The pieces weren't easy to come by, but slowly, after calling in a few favors, Eli had managed to put the puzzle together. He was ninety-nine point nine percent sure his and Char's child was named Damien Martelli. The boy currently resided with his mother, Wanda Johnson, a widow, who had remarried six months earlier. The boy's adoptive father, Anthony Martelli, had been career Air Force. He'd died in a plane crash while on active duty in Iraq two years ago. But what made this scenario so attractive, Anthony Martelli and his wife had lived at Ellsworth Air Force base, near Rapid City, South Dakota, from spring of 1990 to mid-1992.

"Can you believe it? He lives in Seaside," Eli exclaimed, skimming down the map on the screen. "That's only a few hours south of here."

"Well, his mother does," Char said, her excitement noticeably more restrained than Eli's. "You know yourself that family dynamics change when a woman remarries."

He paced to the window of their hotel room. They'd checked in four hours earlier, but the street six stories below seemed as busy as it had at noon. "True. But according to the father's bio, Damien has two younger siblings. And he's only seventeen. I'd put money on him still living with his mother, even if there is a new dad in the picture."

Char had read aloud from Colonel Martelli's obituary, which had been published online in his hometown newspaper. There'd been a fuzzy photo of the fallen war hero's burial in Arlington National Cemetery. A mother and her brood all in black. The tallest of the children was the same height as the woman.

"Do you have a current number for her?" Char asked.

She was sitting at the corner desk, her attention focused on the laptop. Her voice seemed strained.

They'd traded places back and forth all afternoon. Him on the laptop pursuing leads, her on the cell phone making calls. He'd watched her sweet talk and cajole, laugh and fume. He'd lost track of the number of times he'd had to walk into the bathroom to escape the attraction he felt toward her.

Like now. A part of him—a very foolish part— wanted to walk across the room and pull her into his arms. To celebrate. They'd done what they set out to do. They'd cracked the bureaucratic code. They'd found their child—or had a general idea of where and who he was. Weren't they entitled to a couple of high fives and hugs? Maybe a kiss or two?

That was what he wanted. What he did was nothing. Because, damn it, Char deserved better than an emotional basket case looking for any port in a storm. He was a boatload of hazardous waste material rudderless on the crest of a tsunami.

Either that or you're a durn coward.

"No," he said sharply. Not *that* voice again.

She looked at him, her head tilted to one side. "Okay. But Johnson is a pretty common name. Do I start at the top of the list and work my way down?"

"We could try one of the social networking sites. They're really popular with teens. Damien might have a page."

He pushed away from the window and paced to the middle of the room. "Is there a minibar?" he asked, walking to the double doors of a modern black enamel wardrobe.

Her left eyebrow arched questioningly. He knew that look. His grandmother had been a master of it. Without uttering a word she could make him stop dead in his tracks, usually keeping him from doing something he'd later regret.

"Fine. Where's the water you bought?"

They'd made several stops on their trek to the hotel. At a chain pharmacy, Char taught him the tricks of traveling on a budget. "Distilled water is cheaper and better for you," she'd said, handing him a plastic gallon jug. "Compare that to four bottles of fancy label springwater."

He'd tucked the memory away to share with his daughters…if he ever got the chance.

"In the bathroom, next to the glasses," she told him. "I filled the ice bucket while you were on the phone with your friend."

As soon as they'd set up Char's laptop, Eli had called in a favor from an old pal, Travis Turner. The two had met in the Marines. Travis, a self-proclaimed white honky from *Baaaston,* and Eli, the mysterious red man who pretty much kept to himself, had been rivals first, friends second. Travis was now employed by the Department of Defense.

Eli had prefaced his questions with, "Don't ask, *amigo,* but I promise you this is personal and not a matter of national security."

Within an hour, Eli had a list of possible names. A list that included one Anthony Martelli, U.S.A.F. (deceased).

Eli walked into the adjoining room. He almost embarrassed himself by losing the battle with the wrapper on the sealed plastic cup, but he managed to get the cellophane off by ripping it with this teeth. Three giant gulps later, his nerves were starting to settle. Until he looked in the mirror and saw Char watching him.

"What's going on, Eli?"

"I'm not sure I want to do this," he admitted. He hadn't even realized the truth of the words until he said them out loud.

"Do what?"

"Contact the mom."

Char threw out her hands in a what-are-you-talking-about gesture. "We have to go through her. If we show up in Seaside…Oceanside… whatever side and try to find him without talking to her first, we fall into the stalker camp. Not a place I want to be."

He leaned his butt against the tile counter. The hotel was a lot nicer than he'd expected for the price. Char called it a boutique hotel and claimed she got excellent rates because she knew how to bargain. She knew a lot of things he didn't know. But *he* knew what it was like to learn that the child you loved with all your heart belonged to someone else.

"This lady didn't do anything wrong. She doesn't deserve to have this bombshell dropped on her."

Char entered the room and grabbed a plastic cup. With one smooth tearing action, she removed the cover and filled it with water from the jug. "I can see your point, but you're implying that we're a bad thing. Like locust or the plague. Why can't we be beneficial? You said yourself that blending families has its challenges."

She had a point, but he couldn't let go of the memory of the moment when E.J. uttered those terrible words: "You're not my dad."

"You're a dad. You know you can't shield your kids from every bad thing that might happen in their lives. Maybe the bad stuff builds character. Look at me—a bit crazy, but not completely wacko. And I had tons of moments growing up that would have made Dr. Phil puke." She took a drink. "There was this one afternoon when my mom was in her room with her loser boyfriend, whom I loathed. I accidentally set the living-room carpet on fire and— this is where it turns ugly—Devon came running out of the bedroom naked." Her face scrunched up in a way that epitomized disgust. "I honestly believed that men's dicks were little red shriveled things that flapped around like the ear of a beagle."

"There's an image," he said, wincing.

She took a step closer to him. "Fortunately," she said, "you showed up at my aunt's door a year or so later, and I got a more detailed, less-traumatic anatomy lesson."

He groaned and let his chin drop to his chest. "Glad I could help."

Her soft snicker was the only warning he had. "Me, too," she said, suddenly right in front of him. She looked directly into his eyes. "If you hadn't shown up that night, we wouldn't be here now." She paused to moisten her bottom lip. Sexy in an unpracticed way that went straight to his groin. "And, no matter what happens, Eli, I know this is where I'm supposed to be."

He could have argued with her. He had no idea where he was supposed to be. But did it matter? This is where he was. With her. And he'd been fighting this attraction he felt for her ever since that kiss in the parking lot.

Was that yesterday? he asked himself. Why did it feel as though they'd been on this journey for weeks, if not years? Maybe they had been— only far, far apart. Now, they were together.

He put his arms around her and pulled her close. Her body felt small but substantial, if that made any sense. He kissed her. Not fast and hard like the last time. Instead he savored her lips. Warm, wet from the water she'd drunk. Her bottom lip was fuller than the top. Her breath sweet and faintly minty.

"I have to warn you," he said, looking straight into her eyes. "When Bobbi left, she called me an emotional black hole. Are you sure you want to do this?"

She framed his face with her hands and smiled. "What do you get when you combine two emotional black holes together?"

He shook his head. "I'm not an astronomer. I don't know."

"Me, neither, but I'm pretty sure it'll be cosmic."

Was it possible to laugh and kiss at the same time? he wondered. *Hay-yell, yes. Hop to it, boy.*

He froze, his lips an inch from hers. "There's also a distinct possibility that I'm losing my mind."

"I'll pick up any pieces I find along the way. Come on. Let's give the city voyeurs something to blog about."

He had no idea what she meant by that comment, but he let her take his hand and lead in the direction of the two queen-size beds. The corner room had large, double-hung windows, offering a view of the old U.S. Mint across the street. Char had opened the blinds to welcome in the brilliant sunlight that she'd so brilliantly predicted.

The sun had peaked hours ago and long shadows angled through the windows with a sultry golden color. She led him to the end of the bed but didn't sit. Instead she walked to the desk where the laptop sat and purposefully closed the screen.

"This isn't about Damien," she said, glancing over her shoulder. "Agreed?"

Damien. A seventeen-year-old stranger made up of Char and him and the people who had loved and raised him.

As if reading his mind once more, she smiled. "We can discuss whether or not to contact him over dinner. In the meantime, I say we work up an appetite."

His rational mind—the responsible cop who always did the right thing—hesitated. But honestly? What the hell good had that guy ever done for him? Screw responsible. He was going with his gut—or something damn close to his gut.

He leaned back, resting his elbows on the mattress. "Don't you want to close the blinds?"

She slipped off her wool vest then pulled the hem of her black turtleneck sweater out of her jeans. "No, actually, I don't. The last time I stayed here, I was one floor up on the other side of the building, but I remember thinking what I would have done if I hadn't been alone."

She unsnapped the waistband of her pants and slowly lowered the zipper.

Eli got hard from the sound. He shifted sideways so his arousal wasn't quite as noticeable.

She wiggled out of her jeans and neatly folded

them over the back of the desk chair. Her socks disappeared without her even bending over.

His mouth went dry when she turned to face him and started to peel her sweater upward. Pretty white belly. Not swimsuit-model flat. He liked her real woman shape. Her hips were rounded in a good way that fit her physique.

She hesitated a heartbeat before pulling off the top completely, but once she had she dropped it unceremoniously and stood, arms at her side, waiting.

He couldn't move at first. He felt like a kid at Christmas who was given so many toys he didn't know where to begin. But with a nudge from some inner coach, he cleared the distance between them like a predator falling on his prey. She didn't flinch or show any sign of fear.

Instead of kissing her lips, he lowered his mouth to her neck an inch or so above her shoulder and softly sank his teeth into her flesh. Not enough to break the skin, of course, but enough to brand her with his wolf touch.

Wolf. His animal totem, his uncle had told him years and years ago. Some base, primitive part of his mind made room for that alter ego. He swept her into his arms, pleased by the way she fit against his heart. She wrapped one arm around his neck and held tight. The other gripped the material of his shirt.

He carried her to the bed. Not the one she'd selected. He wasn't putting on a show for anyone in this city. If people wanted to watch, they were going to have to work for it. That was as much of an edge as he needed. Good, old-fashioned lust was working just fine as an arousal factor.

"Coward," she said in his ear. Teasing, but breathless.

He liked her breathless.

"We'll see who the coward is when you're naked."

"I can't wait." She wiggled against him. Her breasts, squeezed as they were practically right below his nose, distracted him so much he nearly stumbled over his boots, which he'd kicked off earlier.

He went down on one knee on the mattress. "You're dangerous," he said, kissing her.

"I know," she managed to mumble, despite kissing him back.

Her tongue dueled with his a moment, further distracting him. "Are you going to put me down?"

A flash of heat filled his face. For once, he was glad for his skin tone. "Yes, but I like you like this."

"Like a plate for your dining pleasure?" she asked, referring he supposed to the proximity of her breasts to his mouth. He was certain he detected an edge of cynicism in her voice. He guessed she didn't appreciate her body as the work of art it was.

"Close to my heart."

She pulled back slightly to look him in the eyes. "You mean that?"

He did, but he only knew one way to prove it.

He kissed her again, deeply, exploring the nuances of her mouth, the energy and teasing nature of her tongue. The contact opened him up in ways he'd thought were closed forever. Shut down by pain and disappointment.

I could love this woman. Maybe I already do.

The words came as a revelation, but he managed to keep them to himself. They barely knew each other. They might have made a kid together but that was a long time ago. And even then they'd been strangers. What was happening between them now was physical. For both of them. He was sure of it.

I LOVE YOU, ELI.

Char didn't say the words. Only a fool would admit to a truth that had been a part of her unconscious thought for nearly two decades. The words had been written in indelible ink against pink lined paper in a girlish hand. And that was where they'd stay.

Sex and love were not the same thing. Char's mother had proven that over and over. And Char knew that motive and opportunity only applied in TV detective dramas after the fact. She and Eli were single adults. Well, he was almost single, if what he told her was the truth. So making love wouldn't hurt anybody.

'Cept maybe you, chickadee.

She ground her jaw together to keep from shouting "Shut up." Not exactly the most romantic of phrases.

"Do you want to meet the girls?" she asked Eli. Anything to divert her whack-job mind.

"Pardon?"

She used her free hand to point to her breasts. "They don't have individual names, but I do refer to them as the girls."

He looked faintly shocked.

"Guys do the same thing. One of Mom's boy-friends called his penis Mr. Johnson. Or Mister, for short. No pun intended." She rolled her eyes. "Well, maybe a little one."

His hoot coincided with her butt landing on the mattress. "Char Jones, you crack me up," he said, leaning over as she reclined against the silky spread.

She'd only been half serious about putting on a show for the neighbors. Sometimes she worried that having been exposed to her mother's love life at such an impressionable age might have warped her, but since she was overly selective—her book club friends didn't jokingly refer to Char's home as "the convent" for nothing—she couldn't claim any risky behavior. She was glad Eli had nixed her idea. His choice of bed seemed to signal respect, not prudishness.

She wriggled backward, putting enough space between them that she could reach behind her back and unsnap her bra. She knew there would be lines across her shoulders from the wide straps and an indentation around her middle from the elastic that held every jiggling ounce of her in place. She let the chartreuse lace hang loosely, the flesh still contained by the built-in underwire.

Eli stalked forward on hands and knees until he was once again above her. Dominating but not threatening. He moved with the grace of a wild animal on the prowl. There was a hint of danger in his Paul Newman blue eyes, but when he lowered his head, he went for her straps, not the obvious target.

His nose nuzzled aside first one then the other. She'd learned a long time ago that pretty and functional didn't come cheap, but she'd never been happier with her investment. His tongue tenderly followed the indentation left by the strap, as if trying to erase it.

A flutter unlike anything she'd ever experienced danced in her belly and spread even lower. Her breath went shallow and fast. There was a distinct possibility that she going to have an orgasm without him even touching her magical mystery spot—as her mother called the area.

"What are you doing?"

"Recognizance. Getting the lay of the land, so to speak." He placed his left hand on the other side of her head and leaned across her. His neck was exposed, and inviting. She'd nearly lost it when he bit her. Was she brave enough…?

Maybe, but first she needed to get his damn shirt off. She brought her hands between them and started unbuttoning the first of his Target purchases. She was glad he'd conceded and let her pick out higher-end choices. He arched his back to help her reach the lower buttons. A determined tug brought the tails of the shirt free.

One shoulder, then the next.

"Undershirt. I forgot," she muttered, disappointed…and distracted. It was hard to keep her mind on undressing him when he planted tender, yummy kisses from her shoulder upward to her ear.

Suddenly he sat back. "You're right. I'm way overdressed." He ripped off his black T-shirt, undid his belt and yanked off his pants. Either he wasn't wearing underwear or it came off at the same time. Had they forgot to buy him extra underwear? She couldn't remember. Hell, she couldn't think. Eli Robideaux, the man of her teenage dreams and source of adult fantasies, was naked…on a bed…with her.

"Wow," she murmured.

"Good answer," he said, a twinkle in his eyes. "You're good for my ego. Now, about these remaining scraps of very pretty material…"

She took the hint. Fair was fair. She lifted her hips to permit him to inch down her panties. His look made her breath falter. In a good way. A very good way.

Slowly she sat up and with a quick flip of her wrist, her bra went flying. If anyone down on the street happened to be looking up, they probably got a nice shot of her greenish-yellow bra winging its way across the room.

"Char, my God, you're gorgeous. Lush. Perfect."

The words sounded heartfelt. Almost true enough to believe. The part of her psyche that always felt different from other girls started to heal in a way only love can do.

Maybe not *love* love, but close enough. Enough for her to share her most painful memory.

"I started to *develop,* as my aunt called it, when I was ten. Mom freaked out. She made me stop drinking milk because she read that dairy cows were being given growth hormones that caused girls to mature early. She made me feel like some kind of science project gone amok," she admitted, recalling all too clearly her hurt and embarrassment. "She's the reason I dressed like a bag lady all through high school."

He pressed his nose against her flesh and inhaled. "I'm sorry," he said simply. "But she was wrong. You are beautiful and perfect and I'm the luckiest man on the planet."

Hyperbole. Fantasy. Lies. But healing nonetheless. And even more healing was the way he fondled and suckled, cupped and nuzzled her breasts but didn't make a big deal about them. Then he moved on…lower. He acted as though her breasts were a lovely part of her, but not the defining part.

Char found this liberating, too. In fact, her heart took flight, and the moment he touched her between her legs she was wet and ready. More than ready. She was poised to come.

"I need… Did you bring… Oh, please, tell me we didn't forget condoms," she cried breathlessly, squirming as his finger probed.

"I bought some while you were picking out the water," he admitted, his tone sheepish. "Just in case. It's not like I planned this. Honest."

She could tell he was worried about her response. "I love you," she said, without intending to. "I mean…in a you're-the-smartest-man-on-the-planet-so-how-could-anyone-not-love-you kind of way."

To keep from digging the hole of embarrassment any deeper, she went for a surefire distraction—her mouth on his penis. That worked. She could tell. She might have been afraid to try this in high school but as an adult, she was well-read and had a great imagination. She fearlessly experimented with tongue, teeth and a delicate amount of suction that had him panting in no time.

"Now. Find condom. Now."

He rolled off the bed, dug a small package out of the pocket of his hoodie and returned before Char could savor her triumph. Between the look on his face and the full salute to her foreplay prowess, she knew the best was yet to come.

And she did. Faster than she wanted because she could have stayed in Eli's arms forever, relishing each and every second, each and every taste of redemption. Because that was what sex with Eli was. A life-affirming confirmation that her one impulsive act seventeen years earlier had, in fact, been the right choice.

But if high school had been the wrong time and circumstance for them, was now any better? Lying in his arms, her eyes closed, she tried to ignore the thoughts and worries that came rushing into her mind.

Back then, Eli had been trapped into a marriage that eventually—as of a few months ago—fell apart. His ex-wife had used a baby as bait. What if he suddenly decided Char was doing the same thing? Repeating history, except for the age of the child.

How could she prove she didn't want more when she actually did? She buried her chin against his bare skin and inhaled deeply. She wanted everything with Eli—the sex, the closeness, the comfort and trust and all the rest that came from being with the only man she'd ever loved.

But she couldn't tell him that. Her timing couldn't be worse. Hooking up with a newly divorced guy was a surefire path to heartbreak—her mother had proven that more than once.

No one could predict what would happen when they made contact with their son's adoptive mother, but regardless of the outcome, Char knew that once their quest was completed she would have to walk away. Alone. Because the chances of her and Eli living the proverbial happily-ever-after together were slim to none.

Right?

She waited for the old black woman to confirm that Char was being practical and thinking with her head, not her heart. But her conscience was silent.

Apparently Char was on her own.

Except for Eli.

She quieted her mind to savor the sound of Eli's breathing. She wouldn't gamble on a future with him, but she could dream.

CHAPTER TEN

FOG AGAIN. DAMN, ELI thought, slouching in the passenger seat of the Honda sedan. He hated not being behind the wheel, but Char's credit card got them the rental car and she was the only insured driver. Plus, as she'd pointed out when they left the hotel, she knew the city.

But it was increasingly obvious as they slipped onto the 101 that she wasn't aggressive enough a driver to keep up with the Californians.

"Go faster."

"You are such a guy."

He couldn't argue that—especially not after last night. He'd proven that assertion three times. Three freaking times. He couldn't remember the last time he'd done that. *Or when it had been that good.*

Char Jones was a breath of fresh air. She made him laugh—with her and at himself. She took her gorgeous womanly body for granted. No. Correction. She tolerated her lush womanly body. *The girls* were something to be put up with. Her cross to bear, so to speak.

If they were ever to have a real relationship, he thought, wincing as an SUV cut across their lane, he'd make damn sure she thought better about herself.

A real relationship? What the hell do I know about those?

Damn, he thought, frowning. He almost preferred that wacko, Southern-accented voice to his own conscience, but the truth was he knew squat about love and relationships.

"Stop scowling. I promise to get you to Monterey in one piece."

"I could be in one piece on a stretcher. Dead."

She laughed at his grumpy tone. "I should have let you get more sleep. Sorry."

Eli wasn't. Not about the sex anyway. The call to his ex-wife he could have lived without. While Char was at the front desk discussing rental car arrangements with the concierge, Eli had used her cell phone—with her permission, of course—to check on things back home.

Bobbi's news had been short and far from sweet. "Robert asked me to marry him, Eli. Not right away, naturally. We have to wait for both our divorces to become final, but I said yes. I didn't want you to hear it from somebody else."

Another family screwed up by love. He hated the word.

"What do Micah and Juline think about Robert as a stepfather?"

"They love Robert and his kids. They're a little worried about having to share a room for the rest of their lives, but I promised them we'd get a bigger house eventually."

"What about E.J.?"

She hadn't answered right away. "He's eighteen and mad at the world. You're an idiot. I'm a slut. And Robert is an arch enemy of the state. Remember when you were eighteen and thought you knew everything?"

He remembered his father trying to talk Eli out of marrying Bobbi when he was eighteen. "Just because she's pregnant don't mean you gotta give up all your plans. What if the kid ain't yours?"

At the time, Eli hadn't listened because in his mind there was only one thing to do—the right thing. Pursuing his personal dream had seemed selfish, like something his father would have done. And now the boy Eli thought of as his own had no more respect for him than if Eli had done as his father suggested.

He looked out the window at the oak-dotted hills beyond the urban landscape along the highway. They'd left the hustle and bustle of San Jose behind them and were approaching the town of Gilroy. The sun had come out a few miles back.

"How much longer?"

Char laughed and shook her head. "Get it right. It's 'Are we there yet?' You're a father. You should know that."

"E.J. isn't mine," he blurted out. He hadn't intended on sharing that fact with her. It wasn't a secret any longer, but admitting to the woman who once had a crush on you that you were a chump who got played for eighteen years didn't do much for your image.

She pulled down her sunglasses to glance at him. "Say again."

"E.J. isn't my biological offspring. The genetic markers were close, but not close enough."

"Robert?" she said, her shock obvious.

"Yep. My first cousin's sperm got to the egg ahead of mine." He tried to keep his tone wry but he was pretty sure she didn't buy his cavalier attitude.

"What did Bobbi say?"

"She admitted screwing us both. In her defense, she claimed that she did the math and she was sure I was the father of her baby. But then she was never very good at math and I knew that."

She didn't say anything for a good mile. Finally she said, "That sucks, Eli. I'm sorry."

"Yeah, me, too, but I didn't tell you so you'd feel sorry for me."

"Why did you tell me?"

He rubbed his knuckle back and forth across his chin. "I'm not sure. Maybe so you'd understand that even though I agreed to call this meeting, I'm not trying to replace E.J. I'm still his dad inside. That doesn't stop simply because of a blood test."

"Especially not for a good dad, like you."

Her words were kind, but they actually hurt worse than if she'd said nothing. He'd tried to be a good father, and this was what he got for his efforts. "E.J. hates me at the moment. He thinks I'm a loser, and his mother is a manipulative bitch."

"There were a lot of times I hated my mother," she said. "He'll get over it."

He wanted to believe that, but he and his father had never been close after Eli married Bobbi. Eli hadn't even been there when the old man died.

"And if his mother thinks that our meeting Damien is a bad idea, we're outta there, okay? She didn't do anything wrong, and she shouldn't be punished because your aunt had a sudden glimmer of cognitive lucidity."

She sighed but didn't look at him. "When are you going to believe me, Eli? I don't have some hidden agenda where Damien in concerned. All I've ever wanted was for him to have a wonderful life. But you said yourself that once Mrs. Johnson got over her initial shock, she sounded very open to meeting us." At Eli's insistence, Char had used the speakerphone option when she called Wanda Johnson.

He let his head fall back against the seat, some of his tension easing. Char wasn't Bobbi. Not all women were manipulative schemers. "When are you going to tell me what's in the box?" he asked, only half teasing.

He stretched his neck to see into the backseat.

She'd produced the beautifully handcrafted inlaid wood box out of her suitcase that morning. It was about the size of a ream of copier paper.

"I did tell you…stuff."

Now it was his turn for a droll look.

"Personal stuff. Little things I started saving after… You know, the kinds of things you might put in a baby book. A teeny tiny lock of his hair. Some family photos. My high school graduation program. The grand opening flier from Native Arts."

She shrugged. "I tried to make a family tree, but didn't get too far. Pam flat-out refused to talk about that kind of thing. Marilyn said the past was better left behind us. And Mom didn't know squat about my dad's family."

He was sorry he'd asked. The idea of her saving things for a child she might never meet was sad. Really sad.

"I also included my yearbook because you signed it."

"I signed your yearbook?"

She looked wounded. "You don't remember? Well, why would you? I was Boobs Jones."

He could sense her hurt and he wished he'd been a bigger man, a better man back then. "What did I write?"

"'Good luck, Eli R.'" She gave a soft, sad chortle. "If I told you I slept with it under my pillow for a month, would you laugh?"

If I didn't cry. "No."

"Good. Because I didn't. I was determined not to be like my mother, who wasted way too much time mooning over the wrong men. I had my way with you and planned to forget all about you."

"How long did that last?"

"Until I started having morning sickness."

He didn't know what to say. Fortunately she needed his help reading the map as they came to a fork in the road that would take them west, toward the ocean. Toward the child they made and the family that called him theirs.

"My husband wanted to be here, but he's in court this morning."

Wanda Martelli Johnson wasn't what Char had been expecting. For one thing, she obviously had Native American blood running through her veins. Her long black hair and dark eyes were a clear testament to the fact Char's aunt hadn't lied completely.

But Wanda was also older than Char had pictured. Pushing fifty. Short, round and surprisingly serene, given the fact her son was in jail. Or rather, the hospital.

Damien, the young man Char and Eli were hoping to meet, had been arrested a few days earlier, and while in a holding cell at the juvenile authority, he'd gotten into a fight that landed him in the hospital. "The doctors were worried about a spinal cord injury because he fell on his head. They've kept him sedated, just in case. So far, all the tests have come back clear, thank God."

Eli had called the Johnson home from the highway. Her other children were in school, she'd explained, and her lawyer husband preferred that she didn't invite strangers to their home when he wasn't there. That made perfect sense to Char.

So they'd met at the parking lot of a big-box store visible from the highway then followed her to a small, cheerful café off the beaten path. She hadn't asked for any ID, although Eli had offered.

"Oh, please," she'd said with a weary chuckle, "who on earth would invite themselves to a teenager's messy life if they weren't related by blood?"

That was when she'd explained in detail what she'd only hinted at on the phone when Char first called. "Growing up, Damien was every mother's dream child," she said. "Good grades. A sweet older brother to his two siblings."

She briefly explained that after Damien's successful adoption she and her husband, the Air Force pilot whose obituary Char and Eli had read online, had adopted two more children. A girl from China and a boy from the former Soviet Union.

"Damien was a big help to me. When you're in the military, you move around a lot. Damien is a quick learner and good with languages. He always got the lay of the land before I did. His dad used to call him our scout." Her smile looked wistful.

"But everything changed after Tony's plane went down. We were living in Virginia at the time. My family was back here, and I made the decision to move. Two days after the funeral. Probably not the best timing, but it's hard to think straight when you're in pain. Damien was in school and he had to leave a couple of good friends who meant a lot to him, but…sometimes you have to follow your instincts, right?"

"You have family in the area?"

She nodded. "My parents live in Pacifica. Only a mile or so from the hospital, but they're on a cruise at the moment. Bad timing again," she said. "Not a month after we moved home, my grandfather, whom Damien was quite close to, passed away at the age of ninety-five. That was sort of the last straw for Damien. He seemed to change overnight."

"Drugs," Eli stated, more than asked.

"Ironically Damien's first brush with the law is how I met Steve, my husband. His firm does pro bono consulting for our tribe. He got Damien off with probation and some community service."

Eli asked for details. Char didn't really listen. She could picture her son's spiral into depression all too easily. She might have given up, too, if not for the voice in her head. The old black woman never let Char forget that somewhere out there in the world was a child who might need his birth mother someday.

That day had arrived, but was Char up to the challenge? The only children she had any real contact with were Megan McGannon and Kat's boys. Jordie Petroski was the sweetest little guy on the planet. Char couldn't picture him as a surly, drug-using teen with a chip on his shoulder.

Wanda's voice came back into focus. "Like I said on the phone, ever since this last arrest, I've been praying to the Great Spirit for guidance. Damien is not my little boy anymore. I can't get through to him, and I won't let him bring his anger into our home. His brother and sister look up to him too much. I don't want their relationship with their brother tainted by something that is, I hope, transitory in nature."

Char was impressed. The woman seemed so together and compassionate.

"I feel terrible saying this out loud, but I was prepared to let him go to jail in the hopes that the experience would straighten him out. Steve was afraid that kind of tough love would only add to Damien's anger." She took a deep breath and looked from Char to Eli and back. "And then you called. I believe it's possible the Great Spirit sent you here in our time of need."

Eli pushed his empty cup away and leaned forward, elbows on the table. "In the interest of full disclosure, you should know that I'm on a leave of absence at work because the powers that be were afraid I was going to flip out and shoot someone—namely my ex-wife, who is in the process of taking me to the cleaners. I have three kids who aren't speaking to me at the moment. And I didn't even know Damien existed until three days ago. If he's as street-smart as you say he is, he'll see through me like glass."

Wanda looked slightly taken aback, but Char could tell she wasn't giving up. "What about you, Char? Did you come here to find out about your son and leave well enough alone? Or are you prepared to get involved?"

Char sat up straighter. Eli's shoulder was

almost touching hers. Despite the closeness they'd shared the night before, she knew she was on her own here. As usual. "I've never been married. I'm self-employed. I'm not rich, but I do have a little nest egg saved. If Damien is facing a fine or legal fees, I'd gladly give it to you."

Wanda shook her head. "Money isn't an issue. Tony planned well for the children. Damien has a trust that will be available to him for tuition as soon as he's enrolled in college. If he chooses not to go to school, he can access the money when he turns twenty-five. I'm more concerned that he needs a fresh start…now."

Char gulped. She looked at Eli. His gaze was as inscrutable as ever.

"With your permission, Mrs. Johnson—"

"Wanda. Please."

"With your permission, Wanda, I think Char and I should introduce ourselves to Damien. One thing I know about teens is they hate having people make life-changing decisions on their behalf. He might welcome a change…or he might tell us to take a flying leap."

Char heard the wisdom of experience behind his words. Had that been E.J.'s response to learning he had a new father? Char couldn't imagine what that heart-wrenching revelation must have been like for both son and father.

"That's very profound, Eli. I agree. Why don't

you two follow me to the hospital? I'll clear your visitation with the staff. After you've met Damien, we'll talk again. Hopefully my husband can join us."

Wanda insisted on paying for the coffee then she led the way outdoors. The sky was as bright a blue as Char had ever seen, and the smell of the ocean—once she identified it—was powerful and refreshing. For no reason that made sense, Char felt tears well up in her eyes.

She handed the keys to Eli. So she was the only authorized driver. Big deal. No amount of insurance could cover what was about to happen. Even seventeen years of playing by all the rules wouldn't count for squat if her son rejected her. And why wouldn't he? After all, she'd rejected him first.

"It'll be okay, Char," Eli said, starting the engine.

"What makes you so sure?"

"He's the missing piece, right? Joseph said I was supposed to find him. He's why we're here."

She wanted to believe that, but she knew there had to be a catch. Fate, the Great Spirit, luck, whoever or whatever was in charge of such things had never been on her side. She didn't expect divine intervention to kick in now.

She fastened her seat belt and closed her eyes, expecting to hear the old black woman's take on the subject.

Nothing. That silence worried her almost as much as what was about to happen.

Almost.

CHAPTER ELEVEN

"YOU'RE NOT MY FATHER."

The words still sounded as crisp and fresh and shocking as the day E.J. uttered them. Eli pressed the heel of his hand against his temple to stave off the pain.

For a good fifteen minutes, he'd been sitting alone at the bedside of a young man who appeared to be dead to the world. Char and Wanda, Damien's adoptive mother, had taken off when it had become glaringly obvious that Char wasn't a good waiter.

She'd paced about the bright, pristine private room like a wolf in a kennel. Finally she'd announced, "I need some air." Then she'd dumped her tote bag on Eli's lap and dashed away. He had no idea where she was.

If he craned his neck, Eli could see Damien's mother at the nurses' station going over her son's chart. She seemed like a warm and caring person who had a way of instantly connecting with people. She'd certainly made him and Char feel welcome.

Which, he had to concede, was a little strange. One look at the copy of Damien's birth certificate—or Baby Boy Jones, as the document read—had appeared to seal the deal, as far as Wanda was concerned. She'd accepted Char's word that Eli was Damien's birth father. And here Eli was, poised for a reunion with the child he never knew existed.

"Weird," he muttered under his breath.

The boy on the bed moved restlessly. Eli was usually skilled at estimating a suspect's height and weight, but it wasn't easy when the person was lying in a hospital bed. Still, he guessed Damien to be about E.J.'s height, although a good twenty pounds slimmer.

Probably the drugs, Eli thought to himself, wishing he had a better feeling about how this meeting would go down.

He sat forward, resting his elbows on his knees, hands linked. The kid was good-looking—even with the two-inch square of white gauze taped to his left temple. The nurse had explained that, although they were weaning Damien off the sedatives, they wanted to keep his head immobilized until they were certain there wasn't any swelling.

"But don't worry. He'll be back on his feet in no time. Kids this age are so resilient," the woman had said, in a chipper way.

Fine, Eli thought, but if he was anything like E.J. he was going to be pissed at the world for a long time to come.

The boy's eyelashes flickered against his tanned complexion. His skin tone seemed a perfect blend of Char's fairness and Eli's French-Indian mix. The shape of his eyes made Eli think of Char, although he wasn't sure why. But something about the kid's lips reminded Eli of his father.

He wondered what the old man would have made of this development. He'd had plenty to say when Eli broke the news that Bobbi was pregnant and they were going to get married. "A man spreads his seed. It's nature's way. The woman stays behind and cares for the children. That's society's way. This scholarship is your last shot at a better life, Eli. You can send the kid money once you start making it. Don't let this woman pull you back down."

Eli hadn't agreed about his responsibility to the child Bobbi was carrying. He'd vowed to be a better father than his father had been to him. They'd argued until Eli stormed out of his father's house, hell-bent on getting drunk. The same night of his bachelor party.

And now he got to explain to a kid who didn't know him from Adam—and probably couldn't have cared less—that after his drunken brawl with his son's real father he'd managed to knock up an innocent young girl who was forced to give her child up for adoption. Shit.

"Who are you?"

Eli knew the tone if not the voice. Groggy, with a hint of antagonism. Snarl first; smile only when you must. That was E.J.'s motto, too.

Eli scooted his chair a few inches closer to the bed. "My name is Eli Robideaux. Your mother said she told you about my call last night. I'm someone from your past."

The boy's eyes narrowed. Char again. "You're not my father."

The irony of hearing those exact words from two different boys' lips was not lost on Eli. He gave a sharp, raspy laugh.

"You think this is funny?" the kid snarled. "My dad was a hero. And *Italian*."

The message came through loud and clear but Eli had to ask. "Are you prejudiced against Native Americans?" It hardly seemed likely given his adoptive mother's heritage.

"Don't you mean First Peoples? If you're born here, you're a native."

Smart kid. He probably got that from Char, too. And apparently his anger was universal. "Either way, you have my blood running through your veins."

"I don't believe you."

Eli could have told him about the DNA test Char had arranged for them to take, but instead, he reached down and pulled the Pierre High yearbook out of Char's bag. He flipped through it until he found the header: Seniors.

"Here," he said. "Tell me what you see."

He stood and held the page open with his finger pointing to a mug shot. Eli had gone cheap—the senior special at Sears. No fancy outdoor setting. Just a stark white background that looked almost identical to the pillow resting beneath Damien's head. "Want a mirror?"

Damien looked for a moment then turned his chin toward the door. "Where's my mother?"

"She was talking to the nurses a moment ago. Do you want me to get her?"

"I mean the one who gave birth to me."

"Oh. Char. She went for a soda. I can call her cell phone if you want—"

Damien made a low, raw sound that held an edge of agitation. "I don't want anything from you. I've always known I was adopted. Mom and Dad offered to help me look for my birth parents, but I didn't want to. You had your chance to be part of my life and you chose not to…like…what do I care about you now? Why are you here anyway?"

Eli closed the book. He should have been thinking about how to answer these kinds of questions; instead his mind felt blank.

Show him our chickadee.

Eli's fingers tingled and he quickly flipped back a few pages in the yearbook. The photos of the freshmen and sophomores were smaller, every one with the same background. He ran his finger down the list in alphabetical order. "J…J…Jones. Here she is."

He stepped closer to the head of the bed so he could make sure Damien was looking at the right picture. "This is Char. I think she was fifteen when this was taken. She might have turned sixteen by the time you were born. Too young to raise you on her own. And that's what would have happened because I got married and joined the Marines a few days after Char and I were together."

Damien's thick black eyebrows pulled together but only for a second. It was obvious to Eli that the boy was in pain.

"Let me call the nurse."

"No. Not yet. First, I want to know why. You just screwed her and left? Why?"

Eli hesitated. The truth was ugly and hurtful. He was about to lie when he happened to catch a glimpse of red-orange highlights standing near the interior window. "I don't remember being with Char. I was drunk. It was the night of my bachelor party. I got in a fight with my cousin and he took me to a local nurse—Char's aunt—in case I had a broken nose. Char's aunt was gone. Char took care of me. We had sex."

Blunt, but honest.

"Okay," the kid said. His eyes closed a second later and he didn't stir again—even when the nurse came in to take his vitals.

"Would you mind stepping out?" she asked. "Wound check."

Eli didn't mind at all. In fact, he had half a mind to find the closest bar and disappear into a bottle of tequila.

But he didn't do that. Because when he exited the room Char was there, and without a breath of hesitation she stepped straight into his arms and hugged him. "Good job, Dad," she said softly against his chest. "Good job."

IT WAS CHAR'S TURN to face the music. So to speak. Eli was meeting with Wanda and her husband in the hospital's café, which was situated next to a large, beautiful koi pond. Char had never seen anything like it. The sound of running water was a placid, calming backdrop for the life and death drama many of the people visiting loved ones in the hospital were facing.

She was lucky. Her son—she could almost say the word out loud now—was going to be fine… physically. But Wanda had been adamant that Damien was in bad shape—emotionally and spiritually. "He's like a wounded bird that has to relearn how to fly."

As West Coast goofy as that sounded, Char understood what Wanda meant. Libby once told Char that when Mac was eleven or twelve he found a wounded hawk in an aspen grove. He brought the large bird home and nursed it back to health. "Poor Mac nearly lost a finger," Libby said. "That was one miserable animal and it made sure everyone in the house knew how unhappy it was."

Char could sympathize with what Wanda was going through. The woman's love for Damien was obvious but her concern for holding together her new marriage and protecting Damien's siblings was also apparent. The war had extracted a terrible toll on this family.

But Char knew what it was like to lose a father you worshipped. Maybe, just maybe, she could be of some help to this boy who looked so much like a young Eli.

"What's with the hair?"

His voice was deeper than she'd expected. When she'd eavesdropped earlier, Eli had been doing most of the talking.

"I'm quirky. Ask anyone who knows me," she said, keeping her tone light. Inside her chest her heart was pounding so furiously she was surprised she even had a voice.

He didn't reply but he moved his mouth as if

he needed a drink so she hopped to her feet and picked up the small tumbler with a cap and straw. She shook it to see if there was water in it. Enough. "Drink?" she offered.

"I don't do drugs," he said out of the blue. "I got picked up for selling, but I don't use."

"Why were you selling?"

He gave her a duh look. "Money."

"What do you need money for?"

He fumbled with the straw clumsily but finally got it between his lips and sucked. A couple of long draws seemed to exhaust him. He collapsed back against the pillow.

"I'm gettin' outta here."

She returned the glass to the bedside table. "You needed money to finance your escape. Got it. But…it never crossed your mind to find a job instead of breaking the law?"

His eyes popped open as if he wasn't used to such blunt talk. "I wanna go now. Not ten years from now."

She made a *pffing* sound. "Ten years, huh? Isn't that about what they give drug dealers?"

His expression turned to a scowl. "My mom's new husband is a lawyer. He'll get me off."

Char pretended to be surprised by the revelation. "Oh, I see. This was a test. If the new stepdad goes to bat for you, then you might not hate him quite so much for taking your father's place."

He glared at her but didn't say anything.

"I can do one better. My mom never dated legal professionals so I couldn't run the risk of getting tossed in the Pen—that's what they call the state prison in Sioux Falls—but I devised my own rigorous tests." She scooted the chair closer to the bed as though what she was about to tell him was a secret. "There's the ever-popular trial-by-fire method. But unless you can afford to repaint the interior of your house, I don't recommend it."

Damien's lips flickered a tiny bit but he didn't smile.

"With this other guy she was seeing, I'd set my alarm for 2:00 a.m. then I'd sneak out and let the air out of his tires. For a while he carried a portable compressor with him, but that got old and finally he just stopped coming around."

"Was he a creep?"

Char shook her head. "Not really. But he wasn't Dad, and I was still punishing my mother for the fact Dad died. Not that it was her fault, you understand. It wasn't. But I was angry. And sad. And I was too afraid to have anything to do with drugs. I'd heard whispers that Dad was either high or drunk the night he died. The van he was riding in got hit by a train."

Neither spoke for a few minutes, but Char sensed he wanted to ask her something. Probably the first question she would have asked if their positions were reversed. So she asked it for him. "You want to know why I didn't try to keep you?"

His nod was almost invisible.

"Actually I did," she told him. "I kept you a secret for nearly seven months. You have no idea how hard this was. My mom and I were living in my late grandmother's home with my aunt—a nurse-practitioner. Aunt Pam would have pressured me to get an abortion if she'd suspected the real reason for my weight gain."

His swallow was loud enough for Char to hear.

"But I was determined not to tell anyone until there was no chance of that happening. I thought about running away but decided you needed better prenatal care than you'd get if I was living on the street or in some shelter. I bought over-the-counter vitamins for lactating women. I ate healthy and walked every day. I was in great shape, even though I flunked P.E. after my teacher figured out all the excuses I'd been bringing in were forged."

"Nobody guessed?"

"If you make yourself noticeably different, people actually look at you less closely. They feel embarrassed for you or something. I started wearing kooky clothes. Garage-sale grunge."

"But your aunt found out."

"I started spotting. I was afraid you might come prematurely. It was probably from stress.

Once Mom and Pam found out, the pain and the bleeding went away."

She decided to spare him the details of the horrific fight she'd had with her aunt. Her mother had been more worried that she was going to get stuck raising a second kid, when she'd obviously done such a lousy job with the first. Asking her mother to help care for her child had never entered Char's mind. She'd known what she had to do, and she planned to negotiate the best terms for her baby.

"My aunt had a lawyer friend who would help facilitate a private adoption. She gave me a long list of reasons why this was better than going through a state agency. I believed her. She assured me that you would go to a Native American family. Even though Eli's name wasn't on the official birth certificate, I wanted you to fit in. I also hoped you'd be proud of your heritage."

He made a rude, snorting sound. "Yeah, whatever. My dad's Italian. My mom's half-Mexican and half-Piute. Big deal. The only one who ever talked about that kind of bull was my great-grandpa and he died a couple of months after we moved back. So much for your big plan."

"At least mine didn't land me in jail," she said, sounding way too much like the old black woman.

Damien gave her a dirty look and tried to roll

over. He apparently pinched one of the wires attached to his body because an alarm started to ring and a nurse rushed in.

"Sorry, hon," the woman told Char. "Best let the boy rest a bit."

Char gathered her things and left. She looked around for Eli, but he wasn't in the waiting room. Was he still talking to Wanda and her husband? An uneasy feeling in her gut told her this wasn't a good thing. The last time she'd dealt with a lawyer she lost her son.

But she'd been a terrified young girl at the time. Now she could stand up for herself…and for Damien, if she needed to.

She hoped.

CHAPTER TWELVE

ELI HAD BARELY GOTTEN through the door of the motel room in Carmel before the phone in his pocket started blasting the tune "Baby, Come Back." Grinning, he dropped his backpack in an overstuffed chair and let go of the handle of Char's suitcase. The motel room was quaint, but it wasn't situated close enough to the ocean for him to see water. The concierge at the hospital had arranged for the room at Wanda's behest.

Thinking the caller had to be Char, he flipped open the unit and answered, "Eli here."

"Dad?" A voice he hadn't heard in two weeks.

Eli stumbled over the suitcase and nearly dropped the phone. "E.J.? How'd you get this number? Is everything okay? How are your sisters?"

"Yeah, yeah, we're all fine. But I...um...need to talk to you. I was expecting a woman to answer. Somebody named Char. Who is she, Dad? What's going on? Where are you?"

Questions Eli wasn't prepared to answer. Not

yet. Somehow he'd managed to block almost every aspect of his "other" life out of his mind these past few days. Maybe this was what happened on a real vision quest. Your old world became less real as the new world took shape around you.

But E.J.'s call brought that previous life back into crisp focus. "I'm in California. I had some business to take care of. In fact, I have an appointment with a lawyer in a few minutes. Don't worry. I'm not in trouble. It's old business."

He hadn't expected that explanation to suffice, but it soon became apparent that E.J. had his own agenda and didn't really care about his father's situation. "Dad, things are really f-ed up around here. You need to come back right away."

Can y'all say spoiled?

That voice again. Damn. And she was right. E.J. was spoiled. Damien, too, for that matter. Apparently both had parents who gave too much and expected too little. Either that, or it was their age.

"What's happened?"

"Mom's upset. Really upset. She thinks she might have made a mistake where you and her are concerned. The girls cry all the time. They want to come home. And I've changed my mind about joining the Marines. I'm gonna go to college, after all, Dad."

Dad. Eli walked to one of the windows and pulled aside the frilly curtain. The view opened to the courtyard, which was landscaped to the hilt with pretty flowers unlike anything you'd find in the frozen Midwest at the moment.

"I'm glad to hear that, E.J.," he said, trying to keep any bitterness out of his voice. But a part of him couldn't help recalling E.J.'s last words to him. "A real man would know his own kid, wouldn't he? Is your mother with you, son?" He let the curtain drop.

"Yeah. She…um…just got back from the hospital in Sioux Falls. Apparently Aunt Sue tried to kill herself. Uncle Robert's really broken up over it and the kids are way wigged out."

His cousin's wife had tried to commit suicide? Good Lord. A sick feeling formed in his gut. "Is she okay?"

"Yeah, yeah. She'll be fine. They think it was a play for attention. Right, Mom?" he asked Bobbi, who must have been standing nearby.

Eli wondered what would happen when he broke the news to his estranged family about Damien.

"Put your mom on."

As had been the way throughout most of their marriage, Bobbi spoke, Eli listened. She told him about Sue, who, either accidentally or on purpose, took an overdose of sleeping pills and was in the hospital under a suicide watch.

She confirmed that Robert's four children were pretty "freaked out," as she put it. "I had no idea how much this would impact the kids, Eli. I'm so sorry. When you come back, I think we should try again. For their sakes."

The last was the surefire kicker that always got him to do whatever she wanted, even if he wasn't wild about the idea. Guilt by responsibility.

What could he say? *Sorry, wife and family, I've found a new love. Wait. An old love. And a new kid. I don't need you to make me feel needed and complete.*

"A lot's happened since I left, Bobbi. There isn't going to be a quick and easy fix."

Not the answer his wife had been expecting. Eli could tell by the chilly silence that followed. "You've only been gone, like, five days, Eli. What does that mean?"

"It means I can't picture us picking up again like nothing happened." He told her about Char and Damien as dispassionately as possible.

"Char Jones? I've seen her around Lower Brule. She has funny-colored hair and dresses like a wannabe squaw," she said, using the derogatory word universally hated by Native American women. "I can't believe you slept with her."

In high school and a lot more recently. *A lot more recently.* "Well, apparently, I did. One look at Damien and you know he's my kid, but we've already taken a DNA test to confirm it."

She made a keening sound. "E.J.'s going to be devastated, Eli. He already blames himself for this mess. First, that stupid test blows our marriage out of the water, and now you find out you have a kid with Char Jones. How do you think he's going to take it if you come back with another kid to replace him? Your real son. Good grief, Eli, are you trying to drive him over the edge?"

He sat on the bed, not trusting his legs to support him. He honestly hadn't given his children's reaction to this a great deal of thought. But there was no putting this genie back in the bottle. Somehow they'd all have to get through the rough times ahead.

"What did you expect me to do, Bobbi? Pretend the kid didn't exist?"

"No, but you damn well don't have to bring him back with you. And what about this Char person? Are you involved with her? Have you always had feelings for her—even when you said you were in love with me?"

Eli closed his eyes. He hated this side of Bobbi's personality. Not that she was always self-absorbed, but given the barest hint of a slight against her and she took to chest-pounding indignation.

"I barely knew her in high school. I'm not proud that I had sex with her on the night before my wedding, but it happened. Now I have a kid who doesn't know me, but he has my blood running through his veins. That means he's a half brother to our daughters and a stepbrother to E.J. He's also in trouble. I'm meeting with the local D.A. in a couple of hours to try to figure out some deal to get Damien a second chance."

He paused, then forged on. "If they let me take him out of the state and he comes home with me, you and E.J. and the girls are going to have to work out some kind of relationship with him. Period."

Bobbi remained quiet so long Eli thought they'd lost their connection. Then she said, "Wow, you left home and grew a pair." Instead of snide, her tone was surprised…and a little sad. "Just my luck. You became the man I wanted you to be after I broke up with you."

Eli shook his head. "I'm the same person I always was, Bobbi. Your problem is the grass always looks greener on the other side of the fence, and frankly I'm tired of constantly mending that fence."

He could tell by her silence that she understood exactly what he meant. "Do you want me to tell the kids about Damien? Or do you want to surprise them?"

This time she sounded snide.

"Your call," he said. "You'll do whatever is best for you, Bobbi. I'm confident of that."

"That was uncalled-for, Eli. I made a mistake. Maybe I just wanted more than you could give me. I wanted to be the center of somebody's universe. Is that wrong?"

Eli didn't want to get into mutual recriminations. "We both made mistakes."

"And now you have somebody else in your life. Funny how fast that happened, isn't it? Maybe too fast. Maybe whatever you feel for Char is tied to this boy, who psychologically might be a replacement for E.J. Is Char a replacement for me? She doesn't have to be, Eli. I'll be waiting here to start over, if you want to try."

He didn't reply. He had feelings for Char. Strong, complex feelings, different from anything he ever felt before. But everything between them was new and wobbly and awkwardly linked to a boy who needed them to act like adults and put his needs first. It seemed crazy to think that Eli could make any kind of a life with Char given their past. Was hot sex and a child neither of them had raised a valid basis for a lasting relationship? If he returned home—to an apologetic wife and three upset children—would the emasculated alter-ego Bobbi had so little respect for, Mr. Responsibility, take over?

He didn't know.

"Change isn't necessarily a bad thing, Bobbi. Somebody told me truth and honesty are always the best in the long run—even if they suck right now."

"How profound," she said snottily. "E.J.'s back. Do you want to tell him goodbye?"

He started to agree, but a beep told him a second call was coming in. This one, he could tell from the area code was local. "Sorry, Bobbi. I have another call. I'll keep you posted on what's happening here. Tell E.J. it was good to hear his voice."

She made a rude sound and the line went dead. Eli hit the receive button. As he listened to Damien's mother, he walked to the desk beside the overstuffed chair and switched on the lamp. Pulling a sheet of paper from the drawer, he jotted down directions. He had a meeting in twenty minutes with Wanda's husband and the District Attorney.

CHAR WAS GLAD TO LEAVE the hospital. The long day had taken a toll. She'd decided there was a surreal sense of disconnect that came from being inside a hospital. Days could have passed for all she knew.

"Thanks for bringing back the car in one piece," she said, getting in the driver's seat. "My insurance company thanks you, too."

Eli scowled at her. She liked his scowl. How demented was that?

He stalked around the car and got in. "I told you my insurance is paid up and valid. The only reason I didn't rent the damn car was that my uncle kept my credit card."

That was why she'd agreed to let him drive to the meeting with the lawyer and find them a motel room. She was teasing. He usually got her humor. The fact that he was testy and defensive told her something was going on. The nervous feeling in her stomach returned.

"Which way?" she asked, starting the engine.

"Go back to the main road and head south. The hospital gets a cut rate with a place in Carmel."

"Cool. I've always wanted to visit there. That's where Clint Eastwood lives, I think."

He snapped his seat belt into place then slouched like a sulky teen. Actually he looked a lot like the kid she'd just left in the hospital bed. She couldn't help but smile.

"So how'd the meeting go? Wanda didn't say much." Damien's mother had arrived to relieve Char a few minutes earlier but had seemed a bit evasive when Char asked the same question of her.

"Fine. We were all on the same page, as they say. Even the Assistant D.A. in charge of Damien's case seems to want what's best for Damien."

"So they're not going to charge him?"

He didn't answer right away. He sat forward as if worried that she wouldn't be able to merge onto the road without his help. Odd, she thought. He hadn't second-guessed her driving the entire trip down Highway 101 from San Francisco.

Once the car was up to speed, she glanced at him. "Well?"

He was still frowning. "Apparently California is in the middle of some really intense budget problems. Jails are full and they've had to cut juvenile programs. The D.A. was open to other options."

He motioned for her to take the next exit. Ocean Avenue. She liked the sound of that.

"The Johnsons made it clear that they didn't think Damien should walk away from this scot-free. They felt that would send the wrong message to Damien's friends and siblings. Plus, without some sort of counseling or probation with community service, nothing would change for Damien."

"That makes sense."

"We agreed the best thing was to get him to finish school. And to complete a drug and alcohol program and get regular urine tests to make sure he's not using."

She made the turn. There was quite a bit of traffic, but she wasn't stressed since Eli was navigating. "Damien told me he doesn't do drugs," she said. "He only sold them to make enough money to leave."

"Three blocks ahead on the left."

She glanced sideways. His tone wasn't exactly condescending but she could tell he thought she was being naive. "You don't believe him?"

"In my job, I've learned that most drug users are also very skilled liars."

"You think our son is a drug addict and a liar?"

He shrugged. "I don't know him well enough to say. Neither do you."

She disagreed, but she kept her opinion to herself until they were parked in front of a lovely, upscale motel with some of the most beautiful landscaping she'd ever seen. She turned off the engine and removed the key from the ignition then looked at Eli. The fuchsias could wait. Something was wrong.

"What's going on, Eli?"

He unsnapped his seat belt. "I cut a deal. Maybe not the right one, but I didn't feel like I had a lot of options. Damien broke the law and got in a fight while in the holding cell. He's almost eighteen. Worst-case scenario, they charge him as an adult and he does six months or more with some very unsavory types. Neither of us wants that, right?"

She shook her head. "Of course not, but you said the D.A. isn't going that route."

"Because I gave him an option. I asked if they'd consider letting me take him back to South Dakota if I agreed to become his legal guardian."

That made sense, she figured. Even though Damien would turn eighteen in a few months, in the meantime, it was probably smart to put someone in charge.

"The D.A. liked the fact that I have a background in law enforcement and have a teenage son of my own."

Have, not *had,* as he'd said earlier. "Where do I fit in?"

When he didn't answer right away, her heart stopped beating. "Eli? Tell me you didn't cut a deal that cut me out of the picture."

"Char, you said yourself you have no experience with teenage boys."

"I'm his mother, Eli. You wouldn't even know he existed if not for me. And now you're telling me that because you have a tin star and a y-chromosome you're the best choice to care for this unhappy, messed-up kid?"

"You think he wasn't doing drugs. You want to coddle him. Be the mother you never got to be. He'd trample all over you, Char. Right now, he needs a father."

"That's bullshit, Eli. But even if it were true, why does it have to be one way or the other? Why can't we do this together?"

Another long pause. One that told her they couldn't resolve this sitting in a freakin' car. She opened the door. "Did you get us one room or two?"

He looked at her sharply. "One." He got out, too. "Second floor. Overlooks the flower garden."

She followed him with a growing sense of loss. She wished there was some way to avoid whatever bad news he was about to tell her. Food. Alcohol. Sex. Anything to delay the inevitable.

Am I my mother's daughter or what?

The cackling mirthful response she expected didn't come. "Well…" she prompted her subconscious.

Eli paused to look over his shoulder at her. "Well what?"

"Nothing," she muttered. "Did you say this place had a hot tub?"

"A sauna. Over there."

A quaint blue and red sign hung from the door of the windowless white building that looked as if it might have been a garden shack in an earlier life. "After sitting in a germy hospital all day, I think I'd like to sweat out a bunch of impurities before dinner," she said. "Out with the old, in with the new."

To her surprise, Eli didn't argue. Maybe he wasn't looking forward to hashing out the flaws in his plan any more than she was. Or maybe he was a coward, too.

"The guy who checked me in said they leave robes and disposable slippers in the rooms for guests," he told her after opening the door for her to enter first. "There are supposed to be towels in the sauna room."

She kicked off her shoes and faked a smile. "Sounds like a plan. Are you coming?"

She didn't expect to him to say yes. But once again, Eli surprised her.

"My last sweat lodge was…um…interesting. Yeah, I'm in."

CHAPTER THIRTEEN

"CAN YOU BELIEVE THIS weather?" she asked, grabbing at any conversational straw to ease the tension between them. They'd barely said a word since he returned from the front desk.

Eli acknowledged her question with a grunt much like the one she remembered from that first day when he showed up at her shop. So much had changed, and yet nothing had.

She clutched the two halves of her robe closer to her throat. She knew it was silly to act overly modest after the intimacy they'd shared the night before, but the fact that he'd made plans for Damien without including her meant they weren't together. Not really. That was why she had a large, white bath towel in place under her robe.

Eli had reserved the sauna and gone over the operating instructions with the desk clerk while she took a shower. He still hadn't returned by the time she dried off and faced herself in the steamy mirror, so she'd used the opportunity to ask a few hard questions. Like, what did her son see when he looked at her? A quirky, interesting person who he'd like to know better? Or a kook trying to look quirky and interesting?

It even crossed her mind to buy a box of hair dye the next chance she got and return her multicolored locks to their original hue, if she could remember what her natural color was.

"Ooh, cedar," she said, inhaling deeply as she crossed the threshold of the building. The structure that housed the sauna was larger than it appeared from the outside. There was a chair and narrow table along one wall. Hooks on the opposite wall offered fluffy white towels.

The walls were a soft blue—a color matched by the sky visible through a skylight that put the one in her shop to shame. The glass and cedar sauna unit glowed invitingly. Two white mats were already in place on the bench seat and the digital thermometer claimed the interior temperature was one hundred and fourteen degrees.

She turned to look at Eli. "Did you lock—" She dropped the rest of her question when she saw him slide a metal lever into place. "Thanks."

She slipped off her robe and hung it on a hook above the table, which was stocked with bottles of water and magazines. "Man, they really think of everything." She helped herself to a bottle and backed out of the one-size-fits-all flip-flops she'd found in her room. "Here goes nothing."

Or everything, Eli thought as he watched her step into the ultramodern sauna. He'd never seen the type that used panels in the wall instead of hot rocks and water to create the heat, but the liability release sheet he'd signed had included an informational brochure about the unit. The infrared application sounded highly therapeutic.

But could it fix the problem between him and Char? He doubted it.

He hung up his robe beside hers then wrapped a towel around his waist. He hadn't been surprised by Char's newfound modesty. She was certainly intuitive enough to sense the divide between them. He felt torn in two. And he didn't really like either half of himself.

He slipped inside the brightly lit cedar box and sat on the folded towel a foot to Char's left. She had her eyes closed and appeared to be doing some deep breathing techniques. His gaze lingered over the swell of her bosom above the white towel.

What a jerk! Even with his life in the throes of chaos and upheaval, he wanted her. Even knowing he couldn't promise her squat and might wind up hurting her more than he had in the past, he wanted her.

He squeezed his eyes tight, but blocking one

sense only made him more aware of others. He inhaled deeply to take in the smell of her skin. Soap and something he couldn't quite pin down. Jasmine? Did he even know what jasmine smelled like?

"So you arranged for Damien to walk away with a get-out-of-jail-free card, huh?"

He sat a little straighter, his gaze going to a tiny smudge on the glass door in front of him. "Apparently the state is open to creative ways of cutting their losses where minor offenders are concerned."

"That's good. For Damien, I mean. Will this go on his record?"

He leaned forward to rest his elbows on his knees, weaving his fingers together. The heat felt good but it didn't seem to be sinking in fast enough. In his hazy memory of that night with his uncle, the burning, acrid taste of hot steam had penetrated deep under his skin to short-circuit his brain. Either that or he'd actually experienced an honest-to-goodness vision.

He recalled the chipper, valiant, little, black and white bird that had seemed so sure of itself.

"Eli?"

He blinked as a bead of sweat ran down the side of his face. "Um…sorry. I zoned out a minute. I don't know all the particulars. The D.A.'s office is working on it. Damien and I will both have to sign it, then have it approved by a judge, I believe."

"When?"

He glanced sideways. A mustache of dewy sweat had formed on her upper lip. She brushed it away when she caught him staring. "I don't know. A day or two? Nothing seems to happen very fast around here. Did the nurses say when Damien will be released?"

She retucked the end of the towel above her right breast. "You're asking the wrong person. I'm not family." He could hear the hurt in her tone even though she tried to mask it with a shrug. "Why? Are you in a hurry to return home to an empty house?"

The question took him by surprise. Bobbi had hinted about moving back. She said the girls missed him, missed their life. After eighteen years, she knew which buttons to push. "I... um...I—"

The silence stretched between them as Eli tried to figure out the best way to explain what he didn't completely understand. Why was he such a chump? Why did he feel compelled to take responsibility for a mess that wasn't of his making? Maybe his dad was right. Maybe he was a woman masquerading as a man all these years.

"You're not going home to an empty house, are you, Eli?"

"I'm not sure what's happening back home," he said honestly. He owed her the truth as he knew it. "E.J. called. He got your number from the girl working at your store. He wasn't expecting me to answer."

"Your son called Native Arts looking for you? How'd he know to call there?"

He tamped down the little blossom of pride that he felt. He'd taught the kid a thing or two about investigative work. "I called home from your house, remember?"

She nodded impatiently, her look intense.

"He took the caller I.D. and asked a buddy of mine at work to check it out."

She didn't look impressed. In fact, she looked pissed off. "I can't believe Rachel Grey would give out my cell phone number."

Eli shrugged. He noticed the fact that her gaze went straight to his shoulders and stayed there. Despite her anger, there was desire, too. "He said he sweet-talked a girl who sounded like a real hottie—his words, not mine—into telling him. He convinced her it was a matter of life and death."

"Pia," she muttered under her breath. Her clerk's small disloyalty appeared to trigger a deeper hurt. She seemed to shrink back as if she no longer trusted anyone—especially him.

A sharp sensation pierced the center of his

chest. He hoped to hell he didn't have a heart attack here. He'd signed a paper saying he was in good health. That probably didn't cover emotional pain from impending regrets.

"You talked to Bobbi, didn't you?" she asked.

"Yes. She was with E.J. Apparently Robert's wife attempted suicide. He's rethinking his decision to separate."

"So Bobbi wants the two of you to start over, too."

He rubbed the back of his neck to release some of the tension that had been building since that call. He wanted to say that he didn't love Bobbi anymore—maybe he never had. He wanted to tell Char how much she meant to him. How she'd changed his life in a good way—a great way— in a mere three days. How he wanted her to marry him as soon as his divorce was final.

But he couldn't. He had three—no, four— children depending on him to act like a grown-up. That meant putting their happiness first. Didn't it?

Neither spoke for several minutes. Char broke the stalemate by saying, "Wanda invited me to stay at her house tonight. She offered to show me Damien's baby pictures and videos of him growing up. I—I think I should take her up on the offer."

And he wasn't invited.

"Running away isn't going to change anything."

Her smile seemed reflective. "My friend Libby says you're allowed to make as many mistakes as necessary as long as you never make the same one twice. Spending the night in your arms when you're poised to go back to your wife would probably fall under that category, don't you think?"

He started to tell her he wasn't going back to Bobbi—emotionally. But was that too fine a distinction if Bobbi and his daughters showed up begging to come home? He wasn't the kind of guy to turn his back on his duty.

"I'm sorry, Char."

"Me, too, Eli."

She used the corner of her towel to wipe sweat—not tears, he hoped—from her eyes. A second later, she cleared her throat and said, "But I need for you to understand that regardless of your legal maneuvering, I plan to stay in touch with Damien unless he specifically asks me to go away. I would have liked to be part of the custody agreement, if that's what it's called, but even if I'm not formally recognized, you can't shut me out."

"That was never my intention. I'm trying to do what's best for Damien."

"Since when is having more people who love you a bad thing?"

He didn't have an answer.

When she stood, her towel came loose and for the briefest of seconds Eli was reminded of what he was giving up. Perfection. Goddamn perfection.

"Wait."

He grabbed her free hand—the one that wasn't holding the ends of her towel together at her chest. "Have dinner with me, at least. We can't leave things like this."

Char heard his plea and knew this wasn't easy for him. He wasn't a cavalier jerk who took advantage of her while waiting for his ex to come to her senses. He really was thinking about what was best for his children. And their child, too.

She knew he had no idea how tempted she was to spend one more night in his arms. Her mother would have. Mom would have sacrificed her last scrap of pride to hang on to him, pretending every little crumb of affection he tossed her way was the *real* thing. But she wasn't her mother. And she damn well wasn't cut out to be the other woman in Eli's life.

"I deserve better, Eli," she told him. "If I can't have the whole shebang, then I don't want any of it. Except Damien. With him, I'll take anything I can get."

He squeezed her hand so hard she almost winced. She knew he wasn't trying to hurt her, only to make certain she knew how deeply he believed what he was telling her. "I promise, Char. I'm not trying to exclude you. But simple logistics dictate that I bring him home with me. I have a house and a job. His biological siblings will be there."

She could picture the happy homecoming all too easily. That was why she needed to leave. Now, before she did something stupid, like cry. Or cave in. Or beg him to love her more than he loved Bobbi and his children.

She lifted her chin and purposefully set her shoulders. She felt the towel gap but she didn't care how much he saw. Maybe seeing what he was going to miss out on was fair retribution. "You're the one who came looking for the missing pieces of your life, Eli. There's a damn good chance you found two of them—Damien *and* me. If you're not man enough to make room for both of us in your life, then who needs you? Not me. But you're never going to be able to keep me away from my son. Never."

"That was never my intention. You're not listening to me."

She wasn't a fighter—she'd been exposed to the ugly side of man-woman disagreements almost from day one—but this time she leaned over to get in his face. "When I called Bobbi your *wife* a minute ago, you didn't correct me. You didn't say my *ex*-wife. I'm not my mother, Eli. I don't date, screw or wait around for married men."

She pulled her hand but he countered with a tug that propelled her downward into his lap. His free hand reached behind her head and held her in place so he could kiss her. Hard. As if trying to wipe the words off her lips.

She squirmed to break away but both of them were slick with sweat. As her hands slid over his chest, some signal in her brain turned fury to passion. She didn't even try to fight it. Screw pride. This was Eli. If this was her last hurrah, then she'd damn well make it a good one.

He yanked her towel away with the flourish of a matador. His towel, which was tented at his lap, suddenly disappeared, too. The brightly lit sauna showed every inch of his desire with almost clinical accuracy. Shy, inhibited Char might have been mortified if she weren't so turned on. Need superseded everything else.

She opened her legs and straddled him. His slickness matched hers—everywhere. The outside heat was nowhere near as intense as the inside heat. He let out a low groan that set off a chain of spasms inside her, from her core upward. She shivered with something the exact opposite of cold.

He wrapped his arms around her as he lifted

and twisted to find his own release. "Char," he grunted with a torn sound to his voice. "I love you."

She wrapped her arms and legs around him as if to pull him into the center of her being. His words were a validation she'd been waiting her whole life to hear. Tears formed in her eyes, but she squeezed her lids tight. She didn't want to lose a drop of this moment. This triumph. This redemption.

They stayed that way until one of them—Eli, she thought—moved. "I think the timer went off. It's getting cooler in here," he said.

His voice was low and sexy. She easily could have done this again. Instead she eased back. His hands were still splayed along her rib cage. He hadn't even touched her breasts, she realized. There was an odd satisfaction in that, too, but she didn't dwell on the significance.

"That wasn't supposed to happen," she said, looking into his eyes.

"I know. But I can't take it back."

The sex? Or his declaration of love? She waited a heartbeat or two to see if he'd elaborate. He didn't. Wiggling backward, she planted her feet and stood.

He handed her one of the towels and used the other to clean himself up.

She grabbed her half-empty water bottle then

opened the door. The air temperature was a stark thirty or forty degrees cooler, but she didn't mind. She finally understood how sauna enthusiasts could go from the hot box to the snow pile with apparent rapture.

After drying off, she deposited her towel in a hamper marked Used Towels then put on her robe. Eli was a step behind her. She waited in silence until he was ready, too.

"The concierge gave me the name of a good restaurant right around the corner, if you'd like to eat before we go back to the hospital."

The hospital. Their son. Wanda and the future facing them all.

When they were back in the room, she turned to him and asked, "Did you mean it when you said you loved me or was that sex talk?"

His blue eyes didn't blink or look away—a sure sign of a lie, she'd read. "It wasn't sex talk."

But he couldn't bring himself to repeat it, she guessed.

"I'll shower first," she said, grabbing a few things from her suitcase. She'd have her bag repacked by the time Eli was done getting ready.

Despite sharing the most mind-blowing sex of her life with him, she knew with certainty their happily-ever-after wasn't a sure thing. Eli was a complex person with a history that didn't include her. She'd loved him all her life; he hadn't even known she existed until a few days earlier. But he was right about one thing. They both needed to put Damien first.

She could do that. Even if letting go of today's Eli hurt a thousand times worse than the boy she'd first adored. She didn't try to stop her tears from flowing once she was standing under the shower. They were a freebie—and well-deserved.

CHAPTER FOURTEEN

CHAR CALLED LIBBY from the restaurant while Eli was in the restroom.

"Hi, Lib, it's me. I decided to take you up on your offer. Not Thanksgiving. I can't stay that long, but I thought since I was in the neighborhood…well, um, the state, I'd come see you. Could you meet my train tomorrow?"

"Char, that's wonderful," Libby exclaimed with a little woo-hoo that did Char's bruised heart good. "Jenna and I will pick you up. But why the train? I thought you had a rental car."

"Eli's keeping it. He got someone—" his estranged wife, she assumed "—to fax him a copy of his insurance and his credit card. We were able to take my name off the rental car and put his on. It was impressive to watch. Eli doesn't take no for an answer."

"And you do?" Libby asked with a laugh. "You're the most doggedly determined person I know. It's one of the things I respect and admire most about you."

You do? Before she could ask, though, Libby continued. "Eli…Damien…your few meager text messages have been intriguing me. You're going to tell me everything when you get here, right?"

The inspiration to visit Libby instead of making a fool of herself by hanging around waiting for Eli to come to his senses had struck Char as she walked to her motel room after the sauna. After having breakup sex in the sauna. Something she never in a million years could have seen herself doing. She wasn't sure she recognized herself anymore.

Your friends'll know ya, chickadee.

"It's a long and complicated story, Lib. True fiction, if you know what I mean. Speaking of stories, maybe we could talk about our next book while I'm there. We could call Kat and put her on speakerphone."

They discussed the possibility a minute or so longer, then Char told Libby she had to go because her food was coming. In truth, Eli was returning. But he was like food to her. Nourishment for her soul. However would she be able to go back to her old life without him?

Mebbe you need a new life, chickadee.

"More wine?" he asked, taking the seat across from her. They'd been terribly civil and polite to each other since the moment he stepped out of the shower and spotted her suitcase sitting by the door.

"Do we have time? I don't want to miss Wanda at the hospital."

"She told me she was going to be late because of some function at her younger son's school."

Char put down her napkin. "Damien's been alone all this time? I wish you would have said something becau—"

"Damien's ex-girlfriend was planning to visit. Wanda said this girl was a good influence on Damien when they were dating. She wanted them to have some time alone."

"Oh. Well, then, sure. More wine. You're driving."

The meal at the Flying Fish had been delicious—unlike anything she'd ever experienced before. A Japanese soup that was prepared and cooked *shabu-shabu* style at their table in a clay pot.

"Are you sure leaving now is the best thing? I thought we were in this together."

We were until your ex-wife called and laid a guilt trip in your lap. The word *lap* gave her pause. She cleared her throat and said, "If I'm not a part of the agreement regarding Damien's care and support, then what business do I have hanging around? The court regards you as perfectly capable of transporting him back to South Dakota. Call me when you have a release date and I'll get your ticket switched. I'll even pay for his flight if you want me to."

"That's not necessary. I'll cover it. And I told you I intend to pay you back for everything."

She took a sip of the cold, refreshing wine. "My leaving has nothing to do with money, Eli. You know that."

He didn't reply.

There had been several long silences throughout the meal, but Char was determined to keep things cordial—at least on the surface. She wasn't a crisis junkie like her mother, drawing and redrawing line after line in the sand. No matter what happened between them, she and Eli would need to get along—for their son's sake. Her broken heart was her business.

They skipped dessert, paid the bill and walked to their car, which was parked on the street a few blocks away. She would have loved to stroll along, hand in hand with Eli. Window-shopping, maybe picking up a few souvenirs for the kids, like many of the tourists around them appeared to be doing.

No storybook ending for her.

"I'm sorry if I hurt you, Char. That was never my intention."

He'd stopped in the middle of the flow of walking traffic. She took his hand to pull him to one side. She didn't want to do this in public—even amongst strangers. "I know, Eli. You're a good person. I never doubted that for a minute."

He squeezed her hand. "Don't go."

If he'd included the words *I love you, Char* in that petition, she'd have caved in. But he didn't.

She carefully extricated her hand from his. "I have to. I can't pretend to be happy about the way you're handling this. Damien doesn't need more drama right now. If the situation changes when you get home, you know where to find me." She faked a smile. "Heck, you managed to stumble across my big white teepee when you were on foot and broke. Now, you have my e-mail address and my cell phone number. It's not like we're going back to being strangers."

He didn't dispute that, but he seemed downcast and less sure of himself than usual. A part of her hoped that meant he was questioning his decision to go back to his wife. She wasn't betting on him miraculously making a clean break from Bobbi and choosing Char instead, but she couldn't let go of her dream entirely. Not yet.

"When we get to the hospital, I'd like to talk to Damien alone. If you don't mind."

I MIND, HE THOUGHT. *I mind you making plans without me. I mind you leaving. I mind the fact that I screwed up and now I don't know how to fix things between us.* But he didn't say any of that. He'd lost any right he might have had to try to influence her decisions.

He opened the car door for her then hurried around to get behind the wheel. The rental car was in his name now. He hadn't wanted to call Bobbi again, but given the fact she had a key to his house and knew where he kept his credit card file, his options were limited. Except for that mysterious e-mail, Eli hadn't heard from his uncle. He hoped Joseph still had the contents of Eli's wallet, but he doubted the older man would have been able to figure out how to fax him copies.

Bobbi had responded faster and with fewer questions than he'd expected. Maybe Sue's attempted suicide had had an impact on Bobbi. The two had been friends at one time. A fact that made the difference between Bobbi and Char all the more obvious. He couldn't picture Char faking friendship with a woman whose husband she'd loved for nearly twenty years.

"What are you going to tell him?" he asked, following a string of cars that was turning left onto the main road.

"Goodbye," she said simply.

He fumbled with the control knob for the wipers. A light rain had started.

"Strange weather, isn't it?" she asked, leaning forward to peer out the window. "It's like a fog bank moved onshore."

Her tone was too conversational for his taste.

They'd been utterly civilized during dinner. As polite as strangers.

He hated the way things stood between them, but when he tried to bring up the subject of what might happen in the future, she'd cut him off. He didn't understand that. Bobbi would have talked the subject to death.

"I meant, what are you going to tell him about us?"

"What's to tell? Remember those helium balloons I delivered to the party the first day you showed up at my shop?"

Everything about those balloons had pissed him off at the time. He remembered thinking how frivolous, impermanent and wasteful they were. "Uh-huh," he answered, glad he hadn't said anything to her at the time. He would have come off as Oscar the Grouch. She probably would have beaned him with her talking stick to put him out of his misery. "What about them?"

"Well, if we had released two balloons at exactly the same moment, I guarantee they wouldn't have wound up within five miles of each other. That doesn't reflect badly on either balloon. It simply proves that everyone is subject to the whims of fate. And if anyone happened to reach out and grab one of the balloons' strings, then all bets are off. No one can account for those kinds of variables."

"You're saying I'm full of hot air?"

"No more than I am."

"Are you sure you want to spend the night at Wanda's?"

She nodded with conviction. "I can't wait to see Damien's baby photos." She sighed softly. "I've been waiting seventeen years for this, Eli."

She turned in her seat to look at him. "I used to go to places like Chuck E. Cheese's and the roller skating rink on his birthday. Not because I thought I'd see Damien, but because I wanted to imagine him somewhere like that having fun with his family and friends. Does that sound creepy?"

It sounded so sad he had to make himself grip the steering wheel to keep from reaching out to touch her, comfort her. "Uh-uh," he grunted, his throat too tight to speak.

"Last year, I took Kat's sons to see a 3-D action-adventure movie on Damien's birthday. Afterward, we went out for pizza. It was fun. Almost like the real thing."

He wondered if he would have done the same thing if he'd known about Damien from the beginning. He doubted it. Look at how maturely he'd handled finding out the son he'd raised wasn't his—booze and a half-assed vision quest.

They arrived at the hospital a few minutes later. He drove to the main entrance and stopped. "Go ahead. I'll park the car."

"Thanks," she said. "I didn't think to bring an umbrella. What about my suitcase?"

"I'll bring it with me."

She got out without a backward glance and hurried inside. He drove slowly looking for a parking place. The upper and lower lots were both more crowded than he'd expected given the time of night, but he found a spot under a bright light.

He turned off the engine and sat without moving, his gaze fixed on the shimmering moisture collecting on the windshield. Char was leaving in the morning. He didn't blame her. She had as much right to be Damien's legal guardian as he did. Maybe more. Damien had been in her heart for seventeen years. Ever since his first breath. Eli had spent those years giving his love, attention, hope and heart to other children. His children, but still…

"I'm an ass."

That you are, chickadee.

He put his head in his hands and groaned. The voice was back. Just what his guilty conscience needed—an ally.

"HE'S STILL AWAKE," a nurse—one Char hadn't met before—told her.

They'd exchanged greetings outside the door of the ICU while Char was waiting for the buzzer to sound. "I think they plan to move him to a regular ward tomorrow."

"Really? That means he's improving. Do you know when he'll be released?"

The woman, who had a good ten years on Char, made an offhand motion with her hand. "Hard to say. He developed a slight infection around the wound so he has to stay on IV antibiotics. They're testing it for staph, but we're not taking any chances until the results come back."

Char was glad to know her son was getting the best care available.

Wanda wasn't in the room, as Char had expected. Damien was sitting up, the television remote in his hand. "Hey, Damien, what's new?" she asked, trying to keep her voice casual. She didn't want him to know how difficult it was for her to say goodbye.

There was a sparkle in his eyes she hadn't seen before. "Have you seen this show? It's set in the Black Hills. My sister told me about it but I never watched it before."

She drew up a chair near the head of the bed. "You must be talking about *Sentinel Passtime.* This is going to make me sound like a terrible name-dropper, but my best friend's husband is Cooper Lindstrom."

"No way."

"Yep. And my other good friend, Jenna

Murphy, is engaged to the show's producer, Shane Reynard. She's also a writer on the show. You can check out the credits when it's over."

"Wow. That's cool."

She leaned closer, ostensibly so she could see the TV set, too. In fact, she wanted to absorb as much of his scent as she could.

"Did they actually film this around where you live?"

She nodded. "Yeah. They did a week or so of location work. The film crew was great for business. Honestly they're the reason I could afford to make this trip." She cocked her head, re-alizing for the first time how true those words were. If not for Libby, whose initial contact with Cooper set the entire *Sentinel Passtime* produc-tion in motion, Char might never have met her son.

"Libby—Cooper's wife—is in Malibu at the moment. She lost her grandmother recently and I've decided to visit her, since I'm so close. To cheer her up, you know." Or was it the other way around?

He hit the mute button to silence the commer-cial hawking some wonder cloth that was supposed to absorb a gazillion times its weight. "When?"

She took a deep breath and let it out. "Your mom's going to take me to the train station in the morning. Eli will stay so he can visit you and meet with the lawyers." She tried to keep her tone upbeat. "Hopefully, in a few days you'll be on your way back to South Dakota. Your birthplace."

His frown looked so much like a young Eli her throat closed up and she thought she might weep. "I don't remember it. Dad used to say he was going to take us to the Air Force base where he was stationed when they got me, but he never did."

"Ellsworth. It's in Rapid City. I live about thirty miles from there." She faked a smile. "I'm the only big white teepee in the area. You can't miss my place."

"You're not flying back with us?"

She sensed that the question he was asking was really *What the hell is going on with you and my birth father?* "No. Like I said, I'm going to visit my friends for a couple of days then head home from there. Eli will be your legal guardian. I'm sure he wants to get you enrolled in school as soon as possible. And, of course, you'll meet his family. Your half sisters and stepbrother."

His expression was as inscrutable as his father's. She quickly added, "I do business in Lower Brule all the time, so we'll see each other on a regular basis. My name might not be on that paper, Damien, but I already told Eli that won't stop me from being a part of your life. Only you can do that."

She couldn't bring herself to ask if he wanted her in his life or not. If the answer was no…she didn't want to think about what that would mean to her future, her plans, all the Normal Rockwell moments she'd imagined for her and her son.

Voices resumed on the television. Familiar voices, yet different. Char looked up and spotted Cooper and costar Morgana Carlyle. They were hiking through an aspen grove. She knew the spot. According to Libby, this was the moment she admitted to herself that she had a thing for Cooper. Later that night, Coop and Libby spent the night together and Libby wound up pregnant. Char didn't know if the same thing happened in the script or not.

"Love is a bunch of crap, you know," the young man beside her said.

She snickered softly. "That's always been my take, too, but do you want to know a secret? Something I've never told anybody? I'm a hypocrite. For all my cynicism and bad-mouthing love, I read every romance novel I can get my hands on and I follow all the gossip magazines because I secretly hope that love exists." *Because if it exists then there's a chance I'll get my happily-ever-after, too.*

He didn't say anything. What teenage boy would, she told herself.

She felt embarrassed by her confession. Maybe

she'd made a fool of herself. There was such a thing as too much personal information, she silently chided herself.

"My mom and dad loved each other," he said quietly. "That's one of the reasons I was so mad at Dad for dying. For leaving Mom alone. Then, she met Steve, and it turned out I was pissed off for nothing."

"I hate it when that happens," she said, hoping she sounded sincere, not flippant. "I was mad at my dad, too. First, he divorced Mom and then he died. Unfortunately my mother didn't make as good a choice the second time around as your mother." She put a finger to her cheek, pretending to think a minute. "Or the third. Or the fourth, for that matter."

His grin seemed real. She could see the scared kid behind those familiar blue eyes. She wished more than anything she could offer him a home and a happy life in a picture-perfect world. But she couldn't.

Nobody can do that, chickadee.

She stood. "Well, I'd better go. Eli is going to sit with you until closing time. Hopefully, we'll see each other after you get settled in South Dakota. But you have my cell number and e-mail address. And I'm going to set up a Facebook account as soon as I get home so we can friend each other. In the meantime, just holler if you need anything, okay?"

His chin dipped slightly in acknowledgment. She couldn't tell if he was sad or upset or what. But since there wasn't anything she could do at the moment, she turned to go. "Oh, wait," she said, before she'd taken a second step. "I just finished reading this book. I asked a friend for a recommendation for age-appropriate reading material for a guy who was seventeen going on twenty-five. I read it on the airplane. It's pretty good. What's not to like about having your own personal dragon?"

She handed him the hardcover book with the striking cover. "It's part of a trilogy. If you like it, I'll buy the rest of the books for you."

He studied the back jacket a moment. "Thanks."

"You're welcome." She started to leave again then stopped. "Hey, I know. I'll make *Eragon* my selection for the Wine, Women and Words book club. When it's my turn to host, you can come and be our guest."

"Why me?"

"Well, first, because I'd like you to meet my friends, and, second, because you're the target audience of this book. It would be cool to see if your impression is vastly different than ours."

He gave a shrug.

She decided to take that as a yes. "Later, chickadee," she said. She didn't know why that nickname felt right, but it did.

She also really wanted to hug him, but she wasn't sure he'd be receptive. She settled for giving his hand a quick squeeze. Lame, she knew, and probably cowardly, but hopefully there would be a time in the near future when they could be open and honest with each other.

For the moment, she'd take this gift—she'd finally met and touched the child she'd given up—and treasure it. Anything else that came from this meeting would be pure gravy.

"Okay, then, I'm going. Thanks for not telling me and Eli to take a hike the first minute you met us. I don't have a crystal ball so I don't know how any of this will turn out, but I hope to be a part of your life. That's entirely up to you, of course."

His eyelids were flickering in that way that said he'd be asleep soon. Instead of waiting for an answer, she impulsively dropped a light kiss on his cheek. Scattered patches of stubble competed with a very mild case of acne below where she kissed. One last inhale of his scent and she left the room.

Eli and Wanda were sitting in the waiting room when she entered. It was apparent they'd been talking. Maybe about her. Eli had that discomfited look on his face that she associated with bad news. What could be worse than saying goodbye to the person you'd been waiting so long to meet?

"He's starting to doze off," she said. She retrieved her suitcase from Eli. "I told him my plans and that we'd keep in touch by phone and e-mail once he gets settled."

Wanda stood. She looked tired, but more at peace than she had when they first arrived. Char was glad for that.

"Do you need anything else from me before I leave?" she asked Eli.

His lips tightened, and for a minute she didn't think he was going to respond. Finally he looked at Wanda and said, "Could we have a minute?"

"I'll wait in the lobby," she told Char. "I'm so glad you're going home with me. I hate walking across the parking lot alone."

Char was exhausted, physically and emotionally. The last thing she needed was a big scene with Eli. She put her hand up when he took a step closer. "Eli, please. Let's not drag this out. I knew the risks associated with loving you—I've known them since high school. I chose to ignore common sense and fall back in love with you anyway. That's my problem."

"You're running away."

He raked his hand through his hair. Several strands stuck straight up, like a Mohawk. A deep, wrenching feeling swept through her. To avoid crying, she drew on her anger.

"Well, you did the leaving last time. Now we're even."

"Char, that's not fair."

"Right. Well, we're adults, not kids anymore. We both know fair isn't a constitutional guarantee. Here's the deal, Eli. I'm not going to beg or wheedle or try to guilt you into including me in my son's life. I can take care of myself—I have since I was sixteen, alone and pregnant." She took a step closer and tapped her finger on his chest. "Just don't try to keep me from him. That's all I ask."

Then she left.

Her anger sustained her until she reached the elevator. Then a tsunami of tears formed in the back of her sinuses, nearly choking her. *You can do this, Charlene.* Not the old black woman's voice. Her mother's.

Char didn't know what that meant but it surprised her enough to distract her from her pain. She was back in control by the time she joined Wanda.

"Thank you for doing this," she told the woman who had raised her son. "I can't wait to see pictures of him growing up."

Wanda led the way toward the parking lot. As she'd said, the mist had stopped. The damp chill felt oddly life-affirming. Char didn't bother with a backward glance. The hospital was a convoluted design that was partly below ground. She had no idea where to look to see Damien's room.

But she felt him. In her heart. As she always had. And although a part of her might have wished otherwise, Eli was there, too.

CHAPTER FIFTEEN

"I KNOW TORTURE IS BIG news these days, but I still think a casual roasting of the guy's balls over an open flame seems fitting," Jenna said, setting down her wineglass.

Char grinned. She couldn't help it. Being in the company of friends was more comfort than she could possibly have predicted. In the two hours since Jenna and Libby picked her up at the train station in downtown L.A., the three women had bonded in a way only women could appreciate.

They'd stopped for an impromptu shoe-buying fest, ate fresh crab on the pier and toasted the news of Mac and Morgan's official engagement with two appletini cocktails and a virgin pomegranate daiquiri. They were now nursing wine and water at Libby's Malibu beach house. Alone. Cooper and Shane weren't due back for another hour.

"I appreciate your outrage on my behalf, Jenna, but this really isn't Eli's fault."

"Jenna's right, Char," Libby said, leaning back

in a chaise so her puffy ankles were slightly elevated. Now well into her sixth month, she looked very pregnant. But in a healthy, happy way. "Eli should have included you in the official arrangements. Talk about presumptuous! Just because he's got other kids doesn't mean he's automatically Wonder Dad. If his home life was so great, he wouldn't have been wandering around the Badlands looking for you."

Char and Jenna looked at each other. "Wow, Lib, you're a feisty pregnant woman."

"I think I'm channeling Gran," she said. And just like that her eyes filled with tears.

Jenna reached out and patted Libby's shoulder. "It was like this for me, too, after my dad died. I'd be fine—not even thinking about him—then suddenly I'd start sobbing." To Char, she said, "Coop's worried all this crying is going to have an adverse effect on the baby."

"Do you know what you're having, Lib?"

"Uh-huh. It's either a boy or a girl," she said through her sniffles. "I don't want to talk about it and if Cooper asks you to try to use your influence to get me to change my mind, don't listen to him. Now, Char, tell us about this secret baby you've kept from us for all these years. And we definitely need pictures."

Char took a sip of wine before filling them in on the details she'd glossed over earlier. Jenna seemed particularly moved by Char's story of fighting to keep her baby. "You know, after I was raped, I went through a terrible time of waiting to see whether or not I was pregnant. To be perfectly honest, I'm not sure what I would have done if I hadn't gotten my period. To be that confident about your decision at age sixteen says a lot about the person you are, Char."

Char let her friend's words sink in for a moment. They felt good. And true. She'd never given herself credit for standing up to everyone— even her aunt. "Thanks, Jenna."

"You're welcome. How would you feel about me including your story in a segment of *Sentinel Passtime?*"

Char laughed…until she realized Jenna was serious. "I…um…I don't know."

"Different names, of course. Think about it. You could help me make sure I get the tone right. It might give our younger viewers something to think about. A sort of cautionary tale about the lasting repercussions of impulsive acts." Jenna winced as if realizing her words might have hurt Char's feelings. "Not that that was a bad thing in your case, but…you know what I mean."

Char nodded. "I do. Damien was lucky. His adoptive parents gave him a great life. His first school was in Japan, for heaven's sake. But I think there's a part of him that needed to reconnect with me and Eli to find out why we gave him away. That's the part that breaks my heart. And I can't do anything about it."

Libby shook her head. "You're wrong. You're doing something right now. You're giving Eli and Damien a chance to bond. And when you get back home, you and Damien can work on your relationship. The thing that worries me is what's going to happen with you and Eli."

Char took another sip of wine. She was tempted to get stinking drunk. Maybe she'd light a fire on the beach and do her own, private vision quest. The old black woman and her mother could join her.

"Eli made his choice. He's a good father. Responsible and all that. He has to try to work things out with his manipulative, self-centered, slut of a wife, right?"

She saw the look Libby gave Jenna. Shocked. She didn't know why. "Am I being too blunt?"

"No, you're being Char," Jenna said.

"And we're both glad to see it," Libby added. "For a minute there, we thought Eli put a spell on you."

"The swoo?" Char asked jokingly.

"No," Libby answered firmly. "Swoo is magical."

"Mystical," Jenna chimed in.

"Myopic," Char added cynically.

"That, too. Once Coop put the swoo on me, I was done for," Libby said, obviously pleased with the concept. "What worries me is you got a full dose of swoo back when Eli was seventeen. Forgive the comparison, but Gran always warned that a young rattlesnake was more dangerous than a grown one because they didn't know how to ration their poison."

"You think Eli infected me?"

"Sorta. You've never fallen in love since then, right?"

Char didn't answer. Eli had always been the one. Even when he was someone else's. "So what's the cure? Or am I going to swell up and turn green and slowly rot?"

"Ew," Jenna said, sticking her tongue out.

Libby blanched. "I think I might throw up."

Char laughed. She couldn't help herself. "You two are a hoot. I'm glad you're my friends. How 'bout we agree not to talk about snakes for the rest of the time I'm here? Who needs a refill?"

The sun was slipping behind a fog bank far off on the horizon. The sounds of people on the beach mingled with the steady crash of waves. The air was salty and clean smelling. Char honestly felt as if she could toss her worries up in the air and let the breeze carry them away. Inland. Far, far inland. Maybe all the way back to South Dakota, so they'd be waiting for her when she got home.

"Hey, hey, hey," a familiar voice called from inside the house. "Never fear, dear ladies, the men have arrived. Char, point us toward the dragon you need slayed—"

"Slain," another male voice corrected.

"Whatever, Sir Shane of Lexicon," Cooper put in testily. "We're here and we brought along Sir William. Because he's English and they invented dragons."

"That might have been the Chinese," added a voice with a distinct British accent.

Char looked at her friends and laughed. "Dragons. Snakes. You people really do live in La-La Land. But I like the idea of my personal legion of knights in shining armor. Cool." She lifted her arm and pointed north. "He's thataway, guys. Go get him."

ELI SAT CROSS-LEGGED on the sand, juggling the disposable cell phone he'd purchased. Char had taken hers when she left two days earlier and he'd felt isolated and out of touch without one. He'd intended to call her first thing, but he had yet to hit Send.

"Coward," he muttered.

The midday sand was warm beneath his butt. He wasn't the only person in jeans, but he could tell the natives knew how to dress for this kind of November weather—especially on a Friday afternoon. More layers on top, fewer from the knees down.

Natives.

The word made him want to throw up. A woman in the District Attorney's office told him the reason he'd been given custody of Damien was to circumvent any legal challenge the Native American community might have made if they'd chosen Char over him.

As if his father's tribe gave a crap. For his entire life he'd felt like an outsider. When he first moved in with his father, he overheard someone suggest that Eli was there to take advantage of government benefits.

If they only knew. He sure as hell didn't want that for Damien.

He opened the phone and carefully punched in the numbers he'd memorized. He gazed at the waves gently lapping on the smooth sand of the beach. A few clusters of people were scattered about. Nothing like it would have been in summer, he speculated.

"Hi. You found me. Leave your number and I'll find you next."

He smiled. He hadn't heard her recorded greeting before. He blew out a sigh and closed the phone.

What he needed to say would probably sound lame and pathetic if he tried to leave a message. "Hi, Char, it's me, Eli. The idiot who let you go. I'm sorry. Come back. Please." His jaw tightened.

Maybe if he went for something more positive. "Hi, Char, it's me, Eli. I talked to Bobbi this morning and told her we're going through with the divorce as planned."

Better. But still not exactly right.

"Hi, Char, it's me, Eli. I miss you. I'm pretty sure my life is never going to be right without you. Marry me?"

He stuffed the phone into his pocket. What kind of jerk proposed on the phone while he was still legally married?

He let out a loud sound of disgust and fell backward in the sand. He kept his eyes closed for two reasons: the sun and his eyes were starting to water. From some previously undiagnosed allergies. Or a sudden-onset cold. Not tears. God, no. He refused to cry in public.

He was so wrapped up fighting off his impending embarrassment he almost missed the conversation coming from a few feet behind him—until he realized he was the focus of it.

"Wow, Shane. How'd you do that? Point your finger, pull the trigger and he topples over. That was awesome."

"Why are you looking at me? It could have been William. He was using an imaginary bow and arrow."

"That's what you use on dragons."

The last speaker had an English accent.

"It couldn't have been us. Any projectile—even an imaginary one—would have made him fall forward because we were shooting from behind."

Eli opened his eyes. They really *were* talking about him.

"Then why'd he fall over? Maybe he's on drugs again."

Again?

"He's pissed?"

"How could he be pissed? We haven't even told him who we are or why we're here."

"*Pissed* is Brit for drunk."

"Why can't they talk right?"

"They? You mean me, and I'm standing right here. With an imaginary bow and arrow that I'm going to shove u—"

Eli scrambled to his feet and turned around. Three men were standing a few feet away, looking at him with varying expressions: apprehension, amusement and intense curiosity.

"Who are you?"

They looked at each other, as if trying to determine who would answer. All three were around Eli's height. The blond-haired one looked vaguely familiar. His buddy on his left was dressed all in black. He looked dangerous—in an

I-can-afford-to-hire-a-hit-man way. The third—the Brit, he guessed—was slimmer than the other two and dressed more formally.

"Well?"

The blonde put his hand over his heart in a theatrical manner and bowed. "Sir Cooper at your service."

The dark-haired guy rolled his eyes. "You're not here to serve him, Coop. You're here to avenge his contemptible wrongdoings, remember?"

Cooper. Coop. A light of recognition went off in Eli's mind. This was Cooper Lindstrom. Char's best friend's husband. TV star. Uncle by marriage to the girl whose balloons Eli had carried a week ago.

Had it only been a week?

"Sorry. I got carried away by the role."

The dark-haired guy advanced a step, hand extended in greeting. "You *are* Eli Robideaux, aren't you?"

"Yeah," Eli replied, reluctantly returning the courtesy. They were acting pretty civilized at the moment, but he'd caught that part about avenging something.

"My name is Shane Reynard. This is Cooper Lindstrom and that's William Hughes. We're friends of Char Jones. I'm sure you figured that out."

"Is she still in California?"

"William's flying her home tomorrow. He's a pilot."

"And Morgana Carlyle's agent," the man put in, his accent somewhat less noticeable now.

At Eli's blank look, he tried again. "Coop's ex-wife."

"And costar," Cooper added pointedly. "Why do you always lead with the ex-wife part? Are you going to tell him she's engaged to my brother-in-law, too?"

"I don't have to. You just did."

Eli couldn't tell if the tension between the two men was real or made-up.

Reynard coughed pointedly. "We all went together to buy a small jet. Today was our test flight."

Cooper's expression turned to almost childlike glee. "We all fly back and forth to the Hills so often this thing is going to save us a bundle. Plus, I've always wanted to be able to say I own a jet."

The look William exchanged with Shane was both amused and indulgent. Eli could tell there was true affection between the men. He was envious.

"Could we possibly take this conversation indoors?" the Brit suggested. "Perhaps over tea? Or a pint?"

"A pint of tea? Are you crazy? Talk about

pissing…" Even Eli, who didn't know this guy from Adam, could tell Cooper was joking.

William gave Eli a droll look then started off. "Come along. You, too, dragon."

Dragon? He wondered if this had something to do with the book Char had been reading on the flight out. He didn't ask. "There's a bar right up the street," he told them. He was starting to feel like a regular, sadly.

"So who wants to tell me what this is about?" he asked a short while later when they were seated around a table near the window. The location of the table reminded Eli of his breakfast with Char in San Francisco.

"Well, partly, there was the test-flight aspect," Cooper said, "but we wanted to check you out for ourselves. To see if you're really as big a jerk as Libby and Jenna think you are."

That hurt and he didn't even know these women.

"Am I?"

Shane sat forward, not aggressively, but his focus was intense and a little unnerving. "Too early to tell. But I will say that to someone on the outside looking in, it appears as though you used Char to write this story then cut her out of the final draft."

Eli sincerely hoped the final draft was yet to come, but he wasn't going to admit that to a stranger.

He looked at William, who was drinking from his draft Guinness. "How do you fit in?" he asked. "These two are part of Char's book club, right? But from what I gather, she's the only single member. I don't see a wedding band on your finger."

William held up his left hand for everyone to see. "That is correct and observant. I don't see one on your hand, either."

Not the answer Eli was looking for. If the guy was interested in Char, Eli planned to settle this now.

"Relax, Eli," Cooper said. "William doesn't have a thing for Char. Thank God," he added, rolling his eyes dramatically. "We already have this crazy six-degree of separation thing going with Morgan and Mac."

Shane shrugged. "I've seen worse. Anyway, back to Char and Eli's situation. If you could give us something to take back to the ladies we adore, we'd greatly appreciate it."

"Are you talking a body part?"

Cooper and William laughed. Shane smiled.

"A heartfelt apology might suffice."

William sat forward. "I disagree. Jenna seemed quite bloodthirsty the other night. I think she'd appreciate a fingertip. Maybe part of his ear…"

Cooper patted his pockets. "Anyone have a Swiss Army knife?"

Eli took a large swallow of beer. Talking about his personal life wasn't his way. Especially not with a bunch of strangers, but since these men had Char's ear, he decided to give truth and sincerity a try.

"I'm assuming Char told you about Damien."

All three nodded.

"He's getting the last of his occupational therapy at the moment. He suffered some weakness on his left side as a result of the concussion. With any luck, his doctor will discharge him today or tomorrow." He looked at his watch. "He should be done with his therapy. Do you want to meet him?"

"Sure."

"Great."

"Let's do it."

"Another round?" the thirtysomething server asked. She looked at each of them before suddenly jumping back in surprise. "Oh, my God, you're Cooper Lindstrom. I love you. I watch your show every week. Honey, I don't know what's wrong with the postmaster lady. You could jump in my mail sack any time you wanted."

Several other patrons looked on the verge of coming over. Shane handled the impromptu fanfare with aplomb, and the men were able to slip out a few minutes later, intact.

"Does that happen often?" Eli asked, leading the way to his rental car.

"You get used to it," Cooper said, slipping on a pair of expensive-looking sunglasses.

"The same way you do a venereal disease, I'm told," William added wryly.

"But fame is far less curable," Shane said with a hint of humor.

Eli shook his head in wonderment. Talk about freaking surreal. A week ago he was freezing his ass on the side of a hill in the Badlands of South Dakota and today he was in California, driving Cooper Lindstrom and entourage to meet his and Char's long-lost son.

Could things get any more bizarre?

He froze—his hand an inch or so from the ignition—half expecting the voice to make some snide comment about tempting fate.

"What are we waiting for?" Shane asked.

Eli started the car. "Not a damn thing."

CHAPTER SIXTEEN

"LIBBY, DON'T CRY. PLEASE."

Libby, Jenna and Char were standing in the shade of a metal building that had housed the plane she was about to board. They'd been waiting at the small, private airport for a little over an hour while William, Cooper and Shane went over some kind of checklist. Even from a distance they seemed as exuberant as young boys on Christmas morning playing with their new toy.

"I can't help it, Char. I keep picturing you alone with a frozen dinner on Thanksgiving."

"Don't," Char said. "I'll be fine."

Jenna gave Libby a one-armed hug. "You can't expect Char to hang around here for another week, Lib. She's got a business to run."

Char mouthed a silent "thanks." To Libby, she added, "If I'm overcome by an urgent need for poultry and stuffing, I'll barge in on Kat and the boys. I promise."

Char couldn't explain her almost overwhelming need to get home. Today was Monday—only a week had passed since she and Eli arrived in California. She'd gotten a text message yesterday from Wanda saying Damien was out of the hospital. But Char knew he wouldn't be allowed to leave the state until he and Eli went before a judge. A process that could take days, maybe weeks.

"Don't worry about Lib," Jenna said. "She'll be fine once you're safely in the air. I think she's going through a little separation anxiety. I shudder to think what will happen when her poor kid starts school," she added, leaning down to pat Libby's belly.

Libby brushed her hands away, but in a happy, I-know-I'm-acting-silly sort of way. Char felt a funny tug on her heart. She knew she had a reputation for being less "touchable" than her friends. She wasn't a hugger. But something had changed since Eli came back into her life. She didn't know if she was more comfortable in her own skin or if she felt more deserving of physical closeness, but to everyone's surprise, she walked over to Jenna and Libby and hugged them both.

"Thanks for your support, guys. I really appreciate everything you've done. I mean it. A free trip back—that's sort of above and beyond the call, don't you think?"

Libby sniffled delicately. "I already told you you're doing us a favor."

"Yeah," Jenna added. "It's not that we don't trust William to deliver all this stuff for Kat's wedding safely, but he is a man."

The three looked at each other and laughed.

"Besides," Libby put in, "since you offered to let us use the teepee for the wedding, you can make sure everything is stored where you want it."

Jenna nodded enthusiastically. "And with Rachel there, it just couldn't have worked out better."

Char had suggested using her teepee to hold Kat's wedding to Jack after her third glass of wine two nights earlier. Libby and Jenna had jumped at the offer.

"And leave it to Shane to solve the heating problem," Jenna said, pointing toward the plane. In the light of day the next morning, Char had brought up the issue of her completely ineffectual space heater. "See those four boxes? Patio heaters the studio bought for the shoot he has planned in January. How totally synchronistic, huh?"

Char was impressed. When things fell together that easily, you tended to believe they were fated. Like her trip with Eli to find Damien. Everything went along as if scripted by some divine planner—until Eli pulled the proverbial rug out from under her.

To distract herself from thoughts of Eli, she said, "Did I tell you I talked to Rachel this morning? She's completely revamped my Web site to take advantage of more search engine— What?"

Jenna looked over her shoulder to check on the men then said, "Libby and I think you should sell Native Arts."

Char's jaw dropped. "What? Why?"

"Because you have more to offer the world than someone else's arts and crafts," Libby said, as if carefully picking her words. "You've done a great job with the store, but this might be the perfect opportunity for you to explore some other options careerwise."

Jenna nodded. "Libby said you told her a long time ago that if you had it to do over again you'd become a social worker."

"I did?" Char looked toward the hazy mountains in the distance. She couldn't remember sharing that secret dream with anyone.

Libby touched Char's shoulder supportively. "You'd make a great counselor, Char, because you've been there, done that."

"And Damien is proof you made the right decision," Jenna added.

She looked at her friends for a good minute then opened both arms. "Group hug. You guys are the best, and you've given me something to think about. It's a long flight back. Maybe I'll have a whole new perspective by the time I get there."

"You have your new book club book, right?"

Char patted her purse. "Sounds interesting. Morgana picked it? I like her, by the way. I bet Megan's jazzed about coming here for Thanksgiving."

"We're ready," a masculine voice called.

Char's heart rate escalated a tiny bit. She loved to fly, she reminded herself. And according to Shane, William was a very accomplished pilot. He would, in fact, be flying Libby's brother and niece back to California in a few days.

"So am I," she returned.

And it struck her that she was more than ready. She was eager to get started. She didn't know exactly what the future might hold. Damien. She was fairly certain they'd established a lasting connection. As for Eli? While she wouldn't put money on her odds, she couldn't help clinging to a tiny glimmer of hope that he might eventually return to her. But she wasn't going to mope around waiting. Her friends were right. She had options, and the next great adventure was out there waiting.

"HOW'S THE BOOK?"

Damien was sitting in the window seat. The man on Eli's right was elderly, with a hearing impairment that had been obvious from the moment the flight attendant helped him to his seat. He and Eli had nodded and smiled, but that was the extent of their communication.

So far—about forty-five minutes into their flight—his seatmate to the left had been equally mum.

"Not bad," Damien muttered. "Char gave it to me."

In profile, Eli could see Char's contribution to their son's looks. Damien's nose was shorter than Eli's and tilted slightly upward on the end. And Damien's hair, which was beginning to grow back after being shorn to disguise the large shaved spot around his temple, was a similar color to Eli's but a different texture. Eli was certain he detected some curl, like Char's.

"Did she tell you about the book club she belongs to?"

Damien grunted something that sounded like an affirmation.

"I can't tell you the last non-work-related book I picked up," Eli confessed. "Probably Harry Potter. E.J. really got into that for a while."

They'd finally had the these-are-my-other-kids talk a few nights ago. Damien even visited E.J.'s MySpace page.

Damien turned his chin to look at him. "My dad and I were listening to them when he died. We didn't get to finish the whole series."

"Like books-on-tape?"

"Downloaded. I think the third one's still on my MP3 player." He hesitated. "Do you want to listen to it?"

Eli swallowed. He knew an olive branch when he saw one. "Sure. Why not? I've never listened to an audio book."

Damien reached under the seat in front of him for the worn Miami Dolphin backpack he was using as a carry-on bag. He seemed to know exactly where to find the small silver unit and high-end headphones. The cop in Eli couldn't help but wonder if Damien had purchased them with illicit gains from selling drugs.

"Noise canceling," Damien said, pointing to the logo on the small black earpieces. "Dad got them in Japan the last time he was there. State-of-the-art at the time."

His pride was evident, as was an underlying edge of grief. Eli felt guilty for assuming the worst. He didn't put them on right away. There was so much he wanted to say, but he didn't have the faintest idea how to begin.

So much for the wisdom of making me the guy in charge, he thought, remembering his bitter exchange with Char.

You start by listening, chickadee.

The voice was back. He hadn't heard it in days. Since Char left, actually. Instead of feeling alarmed, he was relieved. He knew at some level that the voice and Char were connected. He didn't know how. He didn't care.

"Your dad sounds like a pretty cool guy," he said. "Didn't you live in Japan, too?"

"Uh-huh. Kyoto. Dad liked to explore places that tourists didn't go. The *real* city, he called it. We ate stuff you were better off not asking what it was because then you'd throw up."

Eli laughed. "I went to Tijuana once, but other than a couple of seedy bars, I can't say I saw the underbelly of the place. I tried menudo though. Do you know what that is?"

Damien nodded, but he didn't look too impressed by Eli's sampling of the lining of a cow's stomach. Eli couldn't remember the flavor or anything about the meal, only that he'd been forced to eat it because he'd lost a bet to his buddy. He gave up gambling after that.

The awkward silence returned. Eli could tell Damien felt it, too, by the way he fiddled with the book cover. Eli picked up the headphones but didn't put them on. "Is there anything you want to ask me? About my…um…life or what to expect when we get home?"

Damien didn't answer right away, then he said, "Your family is Sioux Indian and French, right?"

Eli blinked, surprised. Not the question he'd been expecting. "And Irish, English and German on my mother's side. She grew up in Oklahoma, but her family came from Illinois. She died when I was thirteen. Cancer."

"What about Char's family?"

"You'd have to ask her."

Damien closed his book and leaned down to poke around in his bag a moment. When he sat up he had the box Char had brought with her to give him. A knot formed in Eli's throat as his son opened it. "That's the thing," he said. "She made this family tree, but it's…it's pathetic. It doesn't go anywhere. My dad's uncle researched the Martelli family back to the freakin' Roman emperor times. Look at this." He handed Eli a sheet of parchment with the faint outline of a sprawling oak tree embedded in the paper, each branch identified with a white line for the appropriate name: mother, father, grandparents, great-grandparents.

Not unexpectedly, the paternal side was blank. But the Jones side was equally sparse. Only a few names, with no dates or places of birth included.

He looked at Damien. "Her parents divorced when she was real young and then her dad died. Maybe her mom failed to get that kind of information until it was too late."

"I know, but look," he said, pointing to an empty branch on the Jones side. "She doesn't even know her maternal grandmother's maiden name. That's kinda sad, isn't it?"

Eli agreed, but it felt disloyal to say so. He was about to hand the paper back to Damien when a thought entered his head. A memory. "I met her grandmother once. I think I was a sophomore. We had this gung-ho social studies teacher who made us go out into the community to record oral histories of elderly residents."

"Can you remember anything about her?"

Eli shook his head. "Not really. She was old, of course. And real tiny. Her hair was pure white. She wore it pulled back in a bun, tight to her head, but little curlicues stuck out in places like a dandelion flower gone to seed."

He couldn't believe he could remember that, but the scene seemed to develop in his mind like a photo coming into focus. "We sat in her garden. And I swear, the whole time we were talking these little birds would come and sit on the back of her chair, like they were worried about her or something. It was the weirdest thing I ever saw. That must be why I can remember it."

Damien frowned. "What did she tell you?"

Eli tossed up his hands. "I have no idea. My teacher published everybody's stories in a book, though, and he gave one to each of the people we interviewed. Maybe Char still has it."

"Don't you have a copy?"

Eli snorted. "Are you kidding? I was a jock…in a new school." He hated to admit the truth to a kid who was going to be starting fresh in a new place very soon. "I did my schoolwork and I got good grades, but I didn't tell anyone. It wouldn't have fit with my image."

Damien gave him a sardonic look as if to say "big surprise there, Dad."

"Can I ask you something, Damien?"

"Maybe."

"How come you didn't register on that adoption Web site Char told me about? I mean, you obviously have more Internet skills than me or Char. Weren't you ever curious about the circumstances around your birth or your birth parents?"

Damien shifted uneasily in his seat. He turned his face toward the window for a moment, then finally answered. "I'm not the one who gave their kid to strangers. Mom told me what she knew about my birth mother—too young to keep me and all that, but I figured if I was an accident that nobody wanted seventeen years ago, why would you want me now?"

A painful weight pressed on Eli's chest. He'd made so many stupid mistakes in his life; he really wanted to make the most of this chance. "Have you given any more thought about school?"

Eli had gone over Damien's transcript and had been shocked to see the depth and breadth of the courses his son had taken—and aced—over the years. Damien was not only a brilliant student, but he'd been in an advanced placement track since elementary school. Eli worried that the high school E.J. graduated from the previous June wasn't going to provide the intellectual challenge someone like Damien needed. And Eli knew only too well that a bored kid was a kid who went looking for trouble.

Creditwise, Damien could graduate now. But Eli didn't think that was a good idea. Emotionally, socially, Damien needed another year with his peers. And Eli sure as hell wasn't ready to send his newfound kid off to college when the new semester started.

"Not really. You said I didn't have to decide right away."

"True. But that doesn't mean you can sit around on your duff and do nothing. How 'bout if I give you an assignment?"

Damien looked skeptical. "What kind of assignment?"

"Fill in the missing blanks on this family tree," Eli answered, handing him the paper. "Both sides of the family—Char's and mine. I'll put you in touch with my uncle Joseph. He knows a lot of stuff—just don't let him talk you into smoking *anything*."

Damien smirked. "How am I supposed to find

out about Char's family, if she doesn't know anything? Her mom's dead and her aunt's loopy."

"Not loopy. Pam has Alzheimer's. But there's another aunt. I'll help you find her number." Eli thought a moment. "In fact, *she* might be the one who has that book I was telling you about. I'm sure Char would have mentioned it if she had it. And Pam doesn't seem the type to care about that sort of thing. You can start there."

"Great," Damien said facetiously. But beneath that attitude, Eli sensed a tiny hint of interest.

Eli wasn't sure where this hunch of his would lead, but he hoped it might be the icebreaker he needed to contact Char.

He put on his son's fancy, noise-canceling headphones but didn't start the story. Instead he tried to imagine what he would say to her when he finally saw her again.

"I love you, Char. It took me nearly eighteen years to realize that. Please tell me I'm not too late."

Her answer wasn't a sure thing, but he knew what he hoped she'd say. Soon. Very soon.

CHAPTER SEVENTEEN

"ARE YOU SURE ABOUT THIS?" Char asked as Rachel made the final connections on the Web cam and microphone she'd installed on Char's computer. The gift from Carlinda had arrived a few days earlier with a note that read:

> Your aunt is doing great. The staff at the new facility has given us the green light to open communication with her. I gave high-tech a try and it worked pretty well. Hope you'll have good luck with it, too. Greece is amazing.
> Love, Carly

"Oh, ye of little faith," Rachel said, adjusting the funny little camera perched so it was trained on the person sitting in the chair. "Besides, I backed up all your files on a portable hard drive while you were in California and cleaned up a couple of pesky viruses. Didn't you notice how much faster your computer is working?"

In the week and a half that Char had been home, she'd come to admire Rachel's facility with computers and numbers. More than that she'd come to like and respect Jack's sister. She'd even invited Rachel to join the Wine, Women and Words book club, after running the idea past Libby.

Rachel motioned Char to sit. "If your dementia-inflicted auntie can do this, you have no excuse, kiddo."

With Libby and Jenna in California and Kat stressed about her student teaching and preparing for a wedding, Char had found herself relying on Rachel as a sounding board. "Maybe she's having turkey dinner."

Rachel chuckled. "Nice try, but as you well know, it's earlier on the West Coast, not later. Go on. Boot this puppy up. I want to make sure it works before I leave."

Char sat, but she looked around the store as if hoping for a reprieve. Unfortunately today was Thanksgiving and the shop was closed. "Oh, okay. One quick hi and bye."

Rachel twisted her thick, pretty brown hair into a knot and quickly pulled on a knitted stocking cap. "Wish I could stay. Your conversation with your aunt might be better than *Frost-Nixon,* but my future sister-in-law would freak. I told you my mother was coming, right? Poor Kat."

Rachel had moved out of Char's spare room and into Libby's guesthouse the morning after Char got back. But that first night home, the two women had spent a productive evening talking and getting to know each better after helping William unload the new heaters. Char had half expected to see some sparks between the two, single, extremely attractive and eligible people, but nada, nothing, zip.

"Don't you think William is charming, in a less-bumbling Hugh Grant sort of way?" she'd asked Rachel after her third glass of wine.

"Yeah. He's gorgeous. I was going to say Jude Law-ish. But I am *so* not interested in handsome men. Don't get me started. Lame, bookish, near-sighted, hook-nose, hirsute and hunchback is more my type."

Eventually Char heard about Rachel's bitter, heart-wrenching divorce from her husband—a too-handsome-for-his-own-good pro golfer. Over a second bottle of wine, they'd compared notes on the inequities of romance and bonded.

And yesterday, when Rachel showed up to install a new router just moments after Clive, Sentinel Pass's regular mail carrier, delivered a copy of the Black Hills State Spring Semester course catalog, she became the first to hear about Char's tentative plan to return to school.

"Too bad I can't hire you to manage the store while I'm in class," Char had told her.

"My reformed workaholic brother swears he's only going to work half days once he opens his new practice. Maybe I could sub for you here, too."

Char had been delighted, and hopeful. And on Char's first day back behind the counter, Pia had called to ask for extra hours, citing her desire to pay for acting lessons. With any luck, Char would be able to hang on to Native Arts while she went to school.

She still had the money she'd been saving for Damien, since Wanda convinced her Damien's college costs were covered. But Char didn't feel right using the fund for herself. Having a business to fall back on in case she couldn't make it as a student seemed like the smart way to go.

Rachel looked at her watch. "Ooh, I have to run. Promise me you'll do this. I read an article that said video conferencing with the elderly was really catching on," she said. "But I should warn you, since the person you're talking to is looking at your image on their screen instead of the camera it can be a bit disconcerting. And the voice delay is jarring at first, but you'll get the hang of it."

Char doubted that. "Go. Tell everyone I said hi."

Rachel walked the short distance to the back door. "You're sure I can't talk you into coming with me? It'll be fun…except for the part where I stuff turkey down my mother's throat to keep her from saying something obnoxious about her son marrying a woman he barely knows."

"Poor Jack. Maybe it won't be so bad. All your mother has to do is look at them to see how in love they are."

Rachel nodded so vehemently her stocking cap slid down over her forehead. "I agree, but you haven't met my mom." She readjusted her hat and pulled on her gloves. The same snow that fell the night Eli first arrived was still around. The nights had been long and cold; Char missed him more than she thought possible. "Speaking of love…have you heard from Eli?"

Char rotated her chair to face the computer. "No. But Damien e-mailed to let me know they're in South Dakota. I'm sure I'll hear something soon." *Or I'll hunt them both down and raise a little hell.*

She didn't like being out of the loop where Damien was concerned, but she was trying to give Eli the benefit of the doubt. He'd probably had his hands full since his return.

"Okay," Rachel said with a wave. "I'm outta here. You know where to find us if you get a sudden hankering for turkey."

Once the door was closed, Char sat forward to examine the high-tech-looking little camera.

She felt obligated to give it a try after all the effort Carlinda and Rachel went through to make this happen. A few minutes later, with the help of a nurse's aide who seemed well-versed in telecommunication protocol, Char found herself seated opposite a grainy, far-from-vivid color image of her aunt.

"Hi, Pam. It's me, Charlene. Happy Thanksgiving."

Pam looked the same as when Char last saw her—with one difference. She seemed less anxious—even with a Web cam in her face.

"Happy Thanksgiving to you, too," Pam said. Her tone seemed more like the old Pam, confident and focused. "My sisters and I always called it turkey day because it was hard to feel thankful for much when Daddy was around. He was such a pill."

Char remembered her mother using that phrase to describe some of the men she dated.

"Aunt Marilyn used to say that Grandma was a saint for putting up with Grandpa," Char said conversationally.

Pam seemed to reflect on that comment a moment. "Mama never argued or fought back. She didn't like to draw attention to herself. She was happiest in her garden."

Char had only vague memories of her maternal grandparents, but she pictured her grandmother as a small woman with a gentle touch. "She grew fabulous gladiolas and roses, didn't she?"

Pam's short locks bounced forward and back as she nodded. "That's what I told the boy who called."

Char wasn't sure if Pam was still in the present or slipping into some other plane. She was about to ask, "What boy?" when Pam added, "He said you were his mother. When did you get married? I must have forgotten."

"Damien contacted you? Really? When?" Knowing her aunt had lost all sense of time, she changed her question. "I mean, why? What did he want?"

Pam started to fidget, as if Char's tone made her uncomfortable.

"Sorry, Aunt Pam. I didn't mean to upset you. Do you remember what you and Damien talked about?"

Pam's gaze drifted sideways. Her lips moved but it took a moment for her words to come through on Char's end. "He asked about Mama's family. About them being Negroes. Daddy told me the truth. To be mean. He didn't want me to love her so much. But I did anyway. More than him. That's for sure."

Char shook her head. Now she was positive her aunt had slipped into some parallel universe. Her grandmother wasn't black.

How do y'know, chickadee? She mighta been passin'.

Pam suddenly stood, effectively ending their video conference. Char tried calling her aunt's name but the camera fell sideways and a moment later the attendant leaned down and said, "I think that's it for today. Happy Thanksgiving."

Char's throat was bone-dry and her hands were shaking as she turned off her computer. Talk about unfair. Even if she wanted to check out her aunt's wild assertion, she had no one to call. Her mother was dead and Aunt Marilyn had written a note in her Thanksgiving card saying she'd be ministering to the poor in Helena today.

She paced back and forth, trying to think of someone else to ask. Would Eli's uncle Joseph know?

She grabbed her cell phone off the desk and was in the process of scrolling down to Eli's name when she heard a knocking sound coming from the front of the building. She glanced at the surveillance screen of the parking lot. A large, unfamiliar black SUV was parked in the disabled spot.

Phone open—in case she needed to hit 9-1-1—she started across the room. Two men in parkas were standing in the shadow of the overhang. She recognized them even without seeing their faces. Eli and Damien.

She let out a yelp of excitement and rushed to unlock the dead bolt. "This can't be happening."

Sure it can, chickadee. And it's about time.

She opened the door.

"Happy Thanksgiving," they shouted in far from perfect harmony. Between them rested a large ice chest and they each carried a grocery bag in one arm.

"We brought dinner," Damien said, a mischievous grin on his handsome face.

Char felt so many conflicting emotions she couldn't keep them straight. Shock, surprise, hope, love. And fear. She'd let herself believe in this possibility before.

"What's going on?"

Eli set his bag on the cooler and removed his gloves. "I wanted to call, but I got voted down. It was three to one in favor of surprise."

Three?

"We spent the night with Uncle Joseph and his girlfriend, Mae," Damien explained.

"She lives near Sturgis, remember?" Eli asked. "I was headed there and wound up here."

She remembered their first encounter all too well. She'd relived that wild, impulsive kiss about a thousand times in her mind.

"Okay. So…you were in Sturgis and suddenly decided to surprise me with a Thanksgiving dinner?" She pointed at the cooler. "If there's a turkey in there, I hope one of you knows how to cook it. I'm not exactly Martha Stewart."

Damien juggled the bag in his arms. "Naw. It's a venison roast. Already cooked. Joseph said it was bad manners for Lakota men to go visiting without bringing a gift of food—preferably meat. We got up at dawn to start the coals and do a little prayer ceremony. Wild, huh?"

"At least we didn't have to kill and dress the deer," Eli said. "My bow skills are a little rusty. Not to mention the fact that I don't have a license," he added. To Char he said, "Can we come inside? It's cold out here."

Char stepped back to let them in.

"Cool place," Damien said. "I like the teepee."

She was so overcome by emotion she had to clear her throat twice to be able to speak. "Thanks."

"You're not working, are you?" Eli asked. "We were going to drive around back when we noticed your lights on."

She locked the door behind them. The aroma of roasted meat filled the air, making her mouth water. "I was on the Web cam with my aunt Pam. She told me the strangest thing. I—"

Eli exchanged a quick look with Damien before breaking in. "Sorry to interrupt but Joe wrote out specific instructions about how to finish cooking everything. Can we talk while we take this stuff next door?"

She reached for the bag Eli carried. "Sure. Of course." She spotted two bottles of wine wedged between several plastic containers and a loaf of bread.

"Awesome spears," Damien exclaimed as they wound through the displays. "They could do some damage."

Char stifled a grin. "I'll introduce you to the artist who carves them. How's your hand, by the way? No lingering problems with your fine motor skills?"

"I'm better than a hundred percent. In fact, I'm two hundred percent. Unfortunately some people don't believe that. Some people won't let me drive until I get written clearance from a doctor. Can you believe it?"

The two men argued about law versus common sense and personal liberty the entire time it took to unpack the cooler and the bags. Char loved every minute of the quick-witted, good-natured exchange. She wondered if this was the way real families were supposed to act.

"So, Char," Eli said, handing her the last of the cold stuff to put away while Damien slid the roast into the oven and closed the door. "We wanted to—"

"Wait. Are these cranberries?" she asked, cracking the lid on the small plastic container.

"Yes, but they're made with chipotle peppers. Mae says the recipe is killer with venison."

Char looked at Damien. "Interesting. Learn something new every day."

Damien picked his backpack off the floor where he'd dropped it and said, "Should we tell her now?"

Tell me what? A sudden jolt of panic made her lose her grip on the bowl. It would have hit the floor if not for Eli's quick reflexes. He put the container on the table after giving Damien a scolding look. "Did you set the timer?" he asked. "Joseph was adamant about not letting the meat dry out."

Damien fiddled with his cell phone a moment. "Set. Now can we tell her?"

Eli took her hand, drawing it to his lips as if to reassure her not to be afraid. "Why not? Shall we go into the living room?"

A minute later, they were gathered around her glass and pine coffee table. She and Eli sat beside each other on the couch; Damien was across from them in a chair. "What's going on, guys?"

Eli was about to open the discussion as he and Damien had discussed when he looked at her—really looked at her—and noticed something different. "Charlene Jones," he exclaimed. "What did you do to your hair?"

She lifted her chin defiantly. "I colored it. All one color. It's called Truffle. Jack's sister helped me pick it out. Rachel and I both agreed that if

I'm going back to college to get my degree in social work, I need to look more… um…neutral. I'm already going to be old compared to the other students. I don't want to be weird, too."

He put one arm around her shoulders and hugged her tight. "Oh, love, different and weird aren't the same. Don't you know that, chickadee?"

She stiffened. "What did you call me?"

He took a breath and let it out. "Let me tell you a story. When I was five my mother drove me to South Dakota from Oklahoma and dropped me off at my grandparents' place for the summer, then drove away. I cried for days. My cousins—including Robert—laughed and called me a baby."

"You *were* a baby," she said sympathetically.

"The thing is, even at the age of five, I knew I would never fit in. I had black hair, but blue eyes and pale skin made me different—especially compared to my cousins."

He leaned his face against her palm when she touched the side of his face. "But my grandfather was a very smart man. Instead of ordering the other kids to be nice to me, he told us about a Lakota brave who went to a gathering of tribes to trade buffalo hides for food that his family would need to survive the winter. Unfortunately he got suckered into gambling with some men from another tribe. Before long, he was down to his last hide. If he didn't win, his family would starve."

Eli looked at Damien, who had heard this story on the way here. He'd grudgingly agreed that Char would understand its significance, even if Damien didn't.

"The man was a fool, but a little bird—a chickadee—saved him by pretending to be the playing piece. If it was supposed to be white, the bird flipped one way. If it was supposed to be black, it flipped the other."

"I've never heard that story," Char said.

He shrugged. "I think Grandfather adapted it to fit my needs. Years later, at a powwow, I heard a much more gruesome version. The point is it made the other kids look at me differently. And that gave me a chance to blend in."

She started to say something but he needed to tell her everything. "Even as an adult I've struggled with a sense of identity—white boy from Oklahoma or red man from the Lakota Nation? It took reconnecting with you and meeting Damien to make me realize that I don't have to be one or the other…because I'm both."

"I helped you figure that out?"

He nodded. "Yeah. For one thing, you not only embrace being different, you elevate your uniqueness to a new level. There's nothing black or white about you, Char…" He looked at Damien meaningfully.

"And yet there is," their son said cryptically.

"Pardon?"

Damien reached into his backpack and produced a small, plainly bound book about the size of one of Char's journals. "Your aunt in Montana sent this to me," he said, passing it to Eli.

"Aunt Marilyn?"

Eli flipped to the table of contents page and pointed to his name, which was right below her grandmother's. "I interviewed your grandmother in seventh grade as part of an oral history project."

He handed her the self-published treatise. "I didn't remember anything she said until I reread it. Then it was almost like sitting in the flower garden with her. It's like your journal, Char. Written word trumps inaccurate memory any day. It's all there in black and white."

Damien cleared his throat. "Correction. Your great-grandparents' names are there. It took some serious ass research on my part to get the rest of the facts."

That tingle of awareness she'd felt when she talked to Pam returned. "Are you going to tell me my grandmother's family was black?"

Damien's face fell. "You knew. Eli said you didn't."

"Pam mentioned it this morning. She said you called her, too. I didn't know what to believe. I still don't. Are you sure? Seriously? How is that possible?"

Damien pulled another piece of paper out of his bag and laid it on the coffee table in front of her, this time dropping to his knees on the carpet so he could point out things as he explained what he'd learned.

She put her hand to her mouth in shock. This was the same genealogy chart she'd attempted to fill out when she was Damien's age. No one in her family would tell her anything. Now she knew why.

"Look at all those names and dates. Damien, you're a genius."

He didn't argue the point, but he did add, "Your grandmother's family—the McGruders—pulled out of the area in the Dirty Thirties. She was the only colored person—her words—left behind. She stayed because of your grandfather. I guess she loved him."

She closed her eyes a moment. "But from what Mom and my aunts have said, he was a real bastard. How sad!"

Eli squeezed her hand. "He might not have been very pleasant at the end of his life, but there may have been extenuating circumstances. Your grandmother told me he suffered frostbite during a blizzard when he helped rescue the children at the Checkerboard School—a rural school where six white students and six black students were enrolled. He lost several toes, which meant he was excluded from military service when World War II started."

"And the Great Depression didn't help," Damien said.

Eli nodded. "The only reason they kept their house was because your grandmother took in laundry and boarders."

"Grandma supported the family?" She pulled a face. "That would have been hard on a man of that time's ego."

"You can see why he would have tried to keep her ethnicity a secret. To save face."

"That's sad. Really sad. My poor grandma never got to be who she was because of her husband's bruised ego."

He shook his head. "I think she really loved him, flaws and all."

"Why do you say that?"

"Look at your family tree. She passed away less than a month after he died."

Damien's cell phone suddenly made a loud *ding-dong* sound. He jumped to his feet, proclaiming his need to eat before he keeled over.

Eli held her hand as they walked back to the dining room. They didn't speak, which gave her time to marvel at the strange connection they shared. His grandfather's story that shaped Eli's life. The old black woman's pet name for her. Her grandmother's heritage that provided a missing piece in Char's story. Their son, who was an amalgamation of all those convoluted pieces.

Once they were seated—like a real family—around her table, she lifted her wineglass. "Thank you both for making this the most memorable Thanksgiving of my life."

Eli touched his glass to Char's and waited until Damien's made a faint clinking sound, too. "To the completed circle."

Damien kept the moment from turning utterly maudlin. "Yeah, yeah. I'm starving. Somebody cut the meat."

Eli did the honors with practiced skill and finesse. The smell of roasted meat made her mouth water, but seeing her two favorite men in the world sharing a meal was even more delicious.

Char sampled the wine before filling her plate. "Good wine," she said, passing the green bean casserole her son's way.

"Libby recommended it. I called her to see which kind you like," Eli said.

He made that thoughtful gesture sound like nothing, but she was so touched she could barely swallow her second sip.

"Did Dad tell you I met Cooper at the hospital?" Damien asked, handing her the roasted yams. "He's funny. His two friends were pretty cool, too. William said I might be able to fly their jet someday if I get my license. Right, Dad?"

Dad. She tried not to be envious, but it was hard to control her reaction. Damien must have sensed something because he said, "It's sorta confusing having two mothers. Like, do I call my California mom Mom One and you Mom Two? Or do I keep it simple and call you Char?"

She relaxed. "The latter, thank you." She took a bite of meat swirled in a dab of spicy cranberries. Her taste buds erupted as she chewed. "Oh, my…good meat."

Damien chewed a bite three times as big as hers then swallowed loudly. "Eli, on the other hand, is Dad because I only have one of those. Plus, he gets this grumpy look on his face when I call him Eli." Under his breath, he added, "Probably because E.J.'s being such a jerk."

Char was sorry to hear that. She had a lot of questions but decided they could wait. She didn't want to ruin this pleasant interlude by bringing up harsh reality.

To her surprise, Eli said, "For the record, my divorce will be final in March. Our house is on the market. The girls have forgiven me and are dying to show off Damien to their friends."

Damien whinnied as if he were a prize stud.

"Bobbi and Robert are back together. After her

near-death experience, Robert's wife, Sue, came to her senses and decided she was better off without him."

"Wow," Char exclaimed. "Things have been popping since you got back."

He took a gulp of wine for courage then pushed his plate aside. "That's true. And after careful consideration we've decided that Damien would be happier in a college prep high school with a more urban flavor—relatively speaking—so we're checking out what Rapid has to offer on Monday. I have résumés with a couple of small PDs and the Highway Patrol. Once I tie up the last of those pesky loose ends, I plan to ask you to marry me."

Damien, eyes wide with mock horror, groaned. "Eli. Dad. No. That was the suckiest proposal ever, man. What were you thinking?"

Eli shook his head stubbornly. "What did you expect? Me down on one knee? That's not our way."

"*Our way?* You mean Lakota? But it's not like you brought her a string of ponies, man."

Char fought to keep from laughing. They seemed so serious. She reached out and squeezed Damien's arm, touched that he was fighting for her honor. "It's okay. He brought venison. And my favorite wine. Besides, where would I put a string of ponies? Do you have any idea how much work they'd be? I'm going back to college. I don't have time for ponies."

Eli jumped to his feet. He knew he was going to lose the moment if he didn't do something to regain control. He needed a grand gesture. And Damien was right, the ambience of dirty dishes was definitely lacking. But where…?

You know where, chickadee. What are you waiting for?

The voice. He no longer feared he was losing his mind. He was grateful for the help.

"You win, Damien. Get the doors. I'll bring your mother." He winked at his son as he walked to where Char was sitting, then he bent down and scooped her into his arms.

"Field trip," Damien chortled, bouncing up with far less cool than he usually purported.

They were all in high spirits, joking and laughing, by the time they reached the teepee. Damien quickly fired up the patio heaters William had left. Within seconds, the chill had receded. The natural light that penetrated the heavy canvas embraced them like a comfortable cloak.

Char's heart was thudding in her chest as if she'd run the entire way, instead of being carried. She wasn't afraid, but she knew something momentous was happening and she didn't want to miss a single image to record in her journal.

Eli stopped purposefully, at the exact center of the teepee. Blue sky and brilliant white clouds winked at them through the open cross timbers. He lowered her feet to the floor but kept her close, so when she breathed in she could feel his chest against hers.

"I love you, Charlene Jones," he said, his gaze never leaving hers. "I love the odd, impetuous girl you were when we first met and the strong, self-reliant woman you've become. I would be honored and grateful if you'd love me back, from now until our children's children whisper our story as if it were a myth. Will you marry me as soon as humanly and legally possible? Please?"

"The ring, Dad," Damien prompted.

Eli patted his pocket and a second later pulled out a small velvet box. When he flicked it open, she couldn't contain her gasp. She recognized the artist, Miriam Flies-With-Hawk's, unique style. Finely pounded strands of yellow gold were woven together to create a delicate bird's nest for two beautifully cut stones of onyx and white topaz.

"You're the jewelry specialist," he told her. "You can pick out our wedding bands, but when I saw this, I knew it was you."

She slipped on the ring, which fit perfectly, then touched his cheek with her open hand. "I loved this face in secret from the first moment I saw you. Tall and proud—even a bit cocky," she added, glancing at Damien. "I wish I'd been brave enough to tell you that."

She brushed a tear from the corner of her eye. She'd probably always regret the years they missed out on—both together and with their son—but nothing could be gained by looking back at what was lost. They had a whole future ahead of them.

"I love you, Eli Robideaux. Always have. Always will. And, yes, of course I'll marry you. The sooner, the better. We don't want to be a bad influence on our son."

They kissed. What felt like a second or two to Char must have seemed an eternity for their audience, who politely coughed. Char pressed her cheek against Eli's shoulder and looked at the boy standing a foot or so away. Waiting.

"Come here, chickadee," she said, motioning for him to join them. "You're a part of this family, too."

He did.

The circle was complete at last.

And caught up as they were in their newfound sense of hope and possibility, none noticed their observer. Sitting on the rim of the teepee above them, a small black and white bird watched the humans for several seconds then cocked its shiny head to one side, as if acknowledging its work here was done, and flew away.

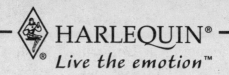

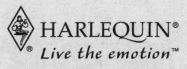

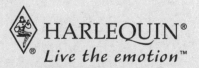

HARLEQUIN®
INTRIGUE®

BREATHTAKING ROMANTIC SUSPENSE

Shared dangers and passions lead to electrifying
romance and heart-stopping suspense!

Every month, you'll meet six new heroes
who are guaranteed to make your spine tingle
and your pulse pound. With them you'll enter
into the exciting world of Harlequin Intrigue—
where your life is on the line
and so is your heart!

THAT'S INTRIGUE—
ROMANTIC SUSPENSE
AT ITS BEST!

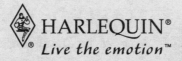

Harlequin® Historical
Historical Romantic Adventure!

*Imagine a time of chivalrous
knights and unconventional ladies,
roguish rakes and impetuous
heiresses, rugged cowboys
and spirited frontierswomen—
these rich and vivid tales will
capture your imagination!*

*Harlequin Historical . . .
they're too good to miss!*

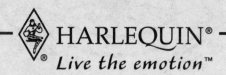